Like Father, Like Son

by
Anne Schraff

Perfection Learning Corporation
Logan, Iowa 51546

Cover Illustration: Michael Aspengren

1   "LISTEN TO THAT howling," Ric Salas said, looking up from the sports section of the *Oceanside Times*. "Maybe that's Tony Robles' ghost moaning again." He chuckled and shook his head.

Ric's younger sister, Eva, was standing by the window looking out. "I think it's just the wind," she said. Early that afternoon a storm had moved in off the bay, and a strong wind had been blowing ever since. "But don't laugh, Ric. Those stories might be true."

"Yeah, right, Eva," Ric said, returning his attention to the sports page. It was yesterday's paper, but he couldn't help reading it again. Most of the section was devoted to the local Friday night football games. One story was headlined, "Junior Ric Salas Carries the Day for Pierce Panthers." Ric proudly clipped the article. He'd had a great season so far as a running back. In the last thirty seconds of Friday night's game, he'd caught a pass and taken it to the end zone for the winning touchdown.

"I wonder how old Robles can keep living in that house with all those silly rumors floating around about his son's ghost," he said, still admiring the article.

"I guess he stays there because that's where his son died." Eva walked to the table and sat down. It was Sunday evening, the time set aside for the Salas children to do their homework.

Ric watched as his younger sister opened her algebra book and started her assignment. Eva's definitely the scholar of the family, Ric thought. He envied her academic abilities. School was easy for her. Ric, on the other hand, was always hanging on to a C by his fingernails.

"*Maybe* Tony died," Ric said. "Robles claims the kid ran away."

Eva frowned. "Yeah, but remember Mrs. Sanchez said she heard Mr. Robles knock Tony down the stairs. She lives right next door to them, you know. And after that night, Tony was never seen again. That was almost ten years ago!"

"Yeah, but there's no proof that he

died," Ric said. "It's not like they ever found a body, you know."

"Well, Mrs. Sanchez thinks he's dead," said Eva. "She's heard his ghost moaning— and she's even seen it." She paused and added quietly, "Sometimes I think I hear it too—late at night."

Ric chuckled again. "Yeah, well, I've never seen or heard a ghost around here, Eva, and I've lived here as long as you have."

Mr. Salas walked by the dining room and glanced in. He always worked hard for everything he had, and he expected his children to do the same. He owned two small restaurants that were doing very well. Five years ago, he had been able to move his family into this house on Linden Street. It was in an older area of town, but the house was nice and exactly what his family needed. Joe Salas was a smart man with big dreams for his children.

"You guys doing your homework?" he asked. Ric quickly put his history book on top of the sports page. He knew his Dad meant was *he* doing his homework. Eva always did hers.

Mr. Salas walked over to Ric. He lifted up the book and frowned. "Is *this* your homework, Ric?" he asked.

"Dad, uh…I just had to take a second to clip this article. I made quite a catch in Friday night's game, you know," Ric said.

"I'm aware of that, Ric. Your mother and I were there, remember? We're very proud of your performance in that game. But, son, football is just that—a game. And there's a time for games and a time for schoolwork."

"Yeah, Dad," Ric sighed. He'd heard this lecture before.

"Well, it's true, son. Football won't get you anywhere in life—unless you're as good as Montana or Marino. Your schoolwork is your future. Do I have to remind you of your midterm report? You're almost flunking American history."

"All right, all right," Ric said. He was sick of the pressures his father put on him about school. Good grades didn't come as easily to him as they did to Eva. And right now, they weren't that important to him. Football was important to him. He'd never mentioned it to his parents, but Ric hoped to be offered a football scholarship to the state university. He figured he didn't need straight A's for that. The scouts from the colleges would be looking more at his playing ability than at his grades. All he had to do for now was not lose his eligibility. And if it weren't for history, he wouldn't even have to worry about that.

As Ric opened his book, he heard the thumping of a basketball on the driveway. He knew his little brother Peter was shooting baskets. Peter was as devoted to basketball as Ric was to football. But Peter was only nine, so the pressure wasn't on him yet. He rarely even had homework. Ric wished he were nine years old again, breezing through fourth grade social studies, instead of seventeen and struggling through American history.

After a few minutes, the sound of the basketball stopped. Peter came running into the dining room, obviously excited.

"Hey, Ric! Look what I found out in the gutter in front of our house," Peter said. He handed Ric a bronze medallion in the shape of a football. On the back of the medallion were the letters *T. R.* and the number *22*.

Ric looked at the medallion. "T. R.? Hmm. Wonder what that means."

"Maybe it's somebody's initials," Peter suggested.

"Could be," said Ric, studying the medallion. "T. R. Wait a minute! Those initials could stand for Tony Robles."

Eva frowned. "Tony Robles?" she asked.

"Yeah," Ric said. "He was an awesome running back a few years ago."

"As good as you, Ric?" Peter asked.

Ric smiled. "Probably not." He reached up and ruffled Peter's hair. "Anyway, I've seen his picture in the trophy case at school. He must have gotten this the year the Panthers took state."

Peter frowned. "You really think so? That it belonged to Tony, I mean?"

"Oh, yeah," said Ric. "Let's see...I think he scored four touchdowns in that game, the most ever scored in a championship game by one player. Boy, he must've really prized this."

Eva looked over. "Mr. Robles probably dropped it," she said. "You'd better give it back to him."

Ric shook his head. "No way! That old man's mean to me. He's been yelling at me for years." Ric imitated Robles. " 'Get off my grass.' 'Keep that football in your own yard.' 'Stay away from that rosebush.' Who knows what he'd do if I gave him this medallion? He'd probably accuse me of stealing it."

Now Peter looked uneasy. "But, Ric," he said, "it belonged to...*Tony.* You sure you want to keep it?"

"Yeah," Eva added, "what if he wants it back?"

"Come on, you guys. Don't be ridiculous. You know there's no such thing as ghosts," Ric answered. "I'm going to keep it—for now, anyway." He turned the medallion over and over in his hand, admiring its craftsmanship. "Man, this is like a trophy."

"I don't know, Ric, maybe you *should* give it to Mr. Robles," Peter said, still troubled.

"Nope. I'm going to wear it around my neck when I play." Ric slipped the medallion onto the gold chain he always wore. "It'll be like a good luck charm."

Eva raised her eyebrows. "Oh, right!" she exclaimed. "You believe in good luck charms, but you don't believe in ghosts? Now who's being ridiculous?"

"Okay, okay," Ric conceded. "Maybe there are such things as ghosts, but that doesn't mean we have one floating around next door." He grinned at Peter. "Hey, Pete, I'll tell you what. When I get *my* medallion for winning this year's championship, you can wear it, okay?"

Peter's worry turned to happiness. "All right!" he grinned, running out the door. A minute later, Ric could hear the sound of the basketball on the driveway again. He closed his history book and sighed.

"Eva, I'm going to my room to read this," he said. "I can't concentrate down here."

"Later," Eva said, without looking up from her work.

But Ric found that reading the assigned pages in his room wasn't any easier. I give up, he thought. Mr. Pike's impossible to satisfy anyway. Who cares about Andrew Jackson's role in the War of 1812? or why people called him 'Old Hickory'?

Touching the medal around his neck, Ric's thoughts returned to Tony Robles. I bet old man Robles didn't appreciate Tony's football triumphs any more than Dad appreciates mine, he thought. Maybe that was what they were fighting about the night Robles pushed Tony down the stairs.

Ric shook his head and considered Mr. Robles. That old man is so weird, he thought. He goes off every day and fishes. Then he sells his fish somewhere, comes home late in that rusty old truck, and hides out in the house. He never speaks to anyone—just yells at the kids in the neighborhood if they step one foot in his yard. And he always wears that straw hat pulled down over half his face. Looks like he hasn't cut his hair in years.

Ric rubbed the medallion between his fingers and whispered, "Help me to the championship, Tony. Then I'll get that football scholarship for sure." A few seconds later, he drifted off to sleep.

Ric woke up around midnight, his history book lying open on the bed beside him and his fingers still wrapped around the medal.

He sat up and stretched, then went to the window. It was starting to storm again.

Ric jumped as a huge clap of thunder shattered the night. Jagged flashes of lightning shot across the sky, and trees waved wildly in the wind. Rain pounded on the roof and against the window. Ric realized he was cold. He undressed quickly and crawled under the layers of blankets on his bed.

As he reached up to turn off the lamp beside his bed, he heard a low moaning sound. It seemed to come from outside. He frowned, his hand suspended in midair. He waited a few seconds, but all he could hear was the raging of the storm. Probably the wind again, he thought.

He turned out the light, sunk down into the soft pillow, and closed his eyes. Again, the sound of moaning drifted through the night. "What the heck?" Ric muttered, swinging his legs over the side of the bed. "If one of those kids is playing a trick on me..."

Ric went to his bedroom door and peered into the darkness of the hallway. He could hear Peter snoring softly in the next room, but other than that the house was quiet. Everyone was asleep.

He went to the window again. Just as quickly as it had come, the storm seemed to be letting up. The lightning and thunder sounded more distant than before. Ric stood in the darkness and listened. Whatever he heard had stopped. Must have been Tony, he said to himself, shaking his head. In his mind he pictured a white-sheeted ghost floating around the neighborhood moaning. No doubt carrying a football, he chuckled.

Ric crawled back into bed, pulled the blankets up around his neck, and slept soundly until morning.

* * *

Monday was bright and clear. It looked as if the storm had moved out for good. On the way to school, Ric remembered that he had not read the assignment for American history.

"I'll study extra hard tonight," he told himself. But in history, Mr. Pike gave a pop quiz over the assignment. It was all about the War of 1812.

"Man, this guy is so unfair," Claudia Evans fumed. Claudia was Ric's girlfriend. Like Ric, she was more interested in athletics than schoolwork. She was captain of the cheer squad and loved it.

As he took the quiz, Ric looked around. Tina Lanza, a smart girl who sat up front, seemed to be breezing through the quiz. But the rest of the class, mostly football players, was really sweating it.

At the end of the period, Mr. Pike handed back the quizzes. Ric's was marked with a big red F. He felt sick. He knew this quiz brought him that much closer to flunking history—and losing his sports eligibility. If that happened, his dreams of carrying the Panthers to the championship were up in smoke. And so was his scholarship.

When the bell rang, Ric went up to Mr. Pike's desk. "Uh…Mr. Pike? I'm sorry I did so badly on the quiz, but I was really busy this weekend, and I didn't have time to study."

"Spare me your excuses, Salas," Mr. Pike said dryly. "We're not even through the first semester, and already I've heard so many excuses I could write a book."

"Mr. Pike, I'm ...worried about flunking this class and losing my eligibility to play football," Ric said.

Mr. Pike raised his eyebrows. "And you should be. If you don't improve your grade in this class, Ric, you can put your football jersey in mothballs."

Ric felt a surge of anger toward the young teacher. He was too hard. His predecessor, Mr. Stephens, would give athletes a passing grade no matter what. What right did Mr. Pike have to deprive Ric of what mattered most to him—playing football?

"Could I maybe do some extra credit to bring up my grade?" Ric asked.

Mr. Pike sneered. "You guys kill me. You goof around in class the whole semester while the rest of the class works, and then you expect to be allowed to do extra credit to bail yourself out. If anybody should be offered extra credit, it should be the serious students, shouldn't it?"

"I guess so," Ric admitted.

"My advice to you, Salas? Study. You've still got time to pull up your grade. Put some effort into the test on Wednesday.

Give that lazy brain as much exercise in class as you give your body out on the football field."

Ric met two other Panthers, Stan Scott and Rafe Thompson, on the way out. Claudia was waiting for him by the door.

"I flunked the quiz too," Stan was saying to Rafe. "Leave it to Pike to stick us with a Monday morning quiz. What a sleazeball! I think he's out to get the football players."

"You think so?" Ric asked.

"Heck, yes. That little wimp wanted to play football so bad when he went to Pierce. My older brother knew him. He says Pike was such a weakling, he couldn't hack it. Never did make the team. Now he wants to spoil our season. Pike hates football players," Stan said bitterly.

"He wants to mess it up for the cheerleaders too," Claudia grumbled. Like the others, she had failed the quiz. As she spoke, her dark eyes glittered with hatred. "We get kicked off the squad if we don't maintain a C average!"

"I'd like to mess it up for him, man,"

Rafe said, his big fists swinging like boulders. Ric felt his own blood rushing. It was pretty obvious. Pike was out to get them.

2 WHEN RIC GOT home from football practice, he tossed his test on his bed and went to take a shower. He didn't think his father would see the test, but he did. Joe Salas was waiting for Ric as he came out of the bathroom.

"An F!" his father cried, waving the quiz in the air. "This is shameful! How could you miss all these questions! Did you even read the chapter?"

"I wasn't having a good day, Pop, that's all," Ric said, avoiding the question. "So I messed up, okay?"

"*Ay!* Not okay! Ric, do you know what my father would do when my brothers and I came home from school with bad grades?" Mr. Salas demanded.

"Yeah, Pop, you've told me a trillion times already," Ric said, shifting his weight from one foot to the other impatiently.

"Well, I'll tell you again. And don't use that tone of voice with me, Ricardo. For every question we missed, my father would make us study for one half hour. Sometimes we were in the house the whole weekend studying. But do you know what? I finished high school with a B-plus average."

"Pop, I do my best in that stupid history class. But Pike's a rat. He couldn't make the football team when he was at Pierce, so now he flunks players out of spite."

Ric's father stared hard at him. "Ric, if there's one thing I've learned in life, it's that you can't blame others for your own failures. If you're flunking that class, it's your own fault. Mr. Pike only gives you the grade you earn."

Mr. Salas paused, then said, "You know, Ric, I almost hope you lose your eligibility. I hope they make you hang up your precious jersey. I know that sounds cruel, but maybe that's what it'll take to make you get serious about school."

As he walked away, he turned and said, "Someday you'll thank Mr. Pike for being the kind of teacher he is. Now I think it's time you opened your book and started studying."

Ric was furious. How could his own father want him to lose something he loved so much! He threw himself onto the bed and opened his history book. All those dull, stupid details! Who could get it straight? Who even cared? The Panic of 1837, the Bank of the United States…it was all so meaningless. Math was better. At least you could use math in your everyday life. But history? What good did it do you to know about things that happened a long time ago?

Stan called after supper. Ric picked up the phone in his room.

"Man, we gotta do something about Pike," Stan said. "After the big test on Wednesday, we'll probably all be off the team."

"Yeah, but what can we do?" asked Ric.

"Rafe's got a great idea," Stan said.

"Oh, yeah? What's Rafe's idea?"

"He's got a cousin over at Lincoln," Stan said, "and they had a teacher like Pike last year. The kids got rid of him."

"Got rid of him?" Ric asked. "How?"

"The guys over there told the principal stuff about the teacher. Like how he let kids get away with cheating on tests," Stan said.

Ric frowned. "I've never seen cheating in Pike's class."

"It doesn't have to be *true*, stupid!" Stan cried.

"Oh yeah, yeah," Ric said. Now he was starting to understand.

"See, the teacher at Lincoln didn't have tenure. That's what they give old teachers so they can't be fired very easily. But new teachers like Pike, they're sort of on probation for the first few years. It's easy to get rid of them," Stan said.

"Anyway," he continued, "the kids hassled the guy too. They egged his house and threw garbage on his lawn. In class, they shot rubber bands at him when his back was turned. He got all rattled and mixed up in his lectures. By the time they were done with him, he was practically begging to leave."

"I don't know," Ric said, shaking his head. "Pike is such a cold fish. I don't think anything would bother him."

"Hey, everybody's got a breaking point, man. You just keep pushing his buttons 'til you hit the right one. We gotta form a tight little group. Let's see. There's me and you and Rafe—he's flunking too. And Claudia and my girlfriend Julie. That's five of us. The rest of the class will probably join in when it starts to get fun, know what I mean?"

"Yeah," Ric said hesitantly. "But I've never done anything like this before, you know. I mean I hate the guy too, but—"

"What're you saying, Salas? That you don't want to do it? Listen, man, you could finish the season as the hero of the Panthers. Don't you realize Pike is gonna blow you out of the game before you even get the chance?"

"Okay, okay," Ric said quickly.

"So we get together this week and decide what we're gonna do, right?"

"Yeah, right," Ric said, hanging up.

"Did anything like what before?" Eva asked. She'd been standing in his doorway eavesdropping on the conversation.

"What are you—a spy?" Ric cried. "Get out of my room, Eva!"

Eva shook her head. "You're such a bozo, Ric. That Stan Scott can get you in big trouble. So can Rafe Thompson. If you guys are cooking up something against Mr. Pike, you're crazy."

"Hey, what I do is none of your business," said Ric.

Eva sighed. "Hit the books, Ric. You're not stupid. You're just lazy. I bet if you applied yourself, you could pull a B in that class."

Ric glared at his fifteen-year-old sister. He couldn't stand it when she acted like his mother.

"Just mind your own business, okay? Do I mess with your life? You're dating that Mike Garcia who looks like a spider monkey, but do I hassle you about it?" Ric asked accusingly.

"You're hopeless, Ric," Eva said. "When are you gonna learn?" She turned and walked off down the hall.

Ric picked up his history book again. Against his will, he read chapter four. Then he read it again. He took notes on what he thought were the important parts. Then he studied his notes. He hated every minute of it, but he did it.

Around midnight he closed the book.

He went to the window and stretched. It was nice to see the moon again shedding a milky brightness over the neighborhood. Glancing down, he saw Mr. Robles in his backyard. From Ric's angle, all he could see was the top of the old man's straw hat. Doesn't he ever take that thing off? Ric wondered.

Mr. Robles was standing before his rosebush. It was the only flowering shrub in the entire yard. Suddenly, Mr. Robles dropped to his knees in front of the bush and covered his face with his hands. Ric could see his shoulders shaking.

"Man alive!" Ric said to himself. "He's crying!"

Ric's first reaction was sympathy. To still be crying like that over a son gone for ten years is really sad, Ric thought. But then his heart hardened toward his neighbor. He could imagine what it must have been like for poor Tony living under his father's harsh thumb.

"You brought your grief upon yourself, old man," Ric muttered. "Why'd you knock your son down the stairs, anyway? Wasn't he smart enough for you? Did he love football too much? I don't blame him for running away. Sometimes I wish I could do the same."

Ric began to wonder what had really happened that night. What had they fought about?

He remembered Mrs. Sanchez telling his mother her version of the story shortly after his family had moved in. She remembered it all—the yelling and screaming, the fighting.

"Like two scorpions in a bottle," the older woman had told Mrs. Salas one day over coffee. "Mrs. Robles died shortly after Tony was born, so there was no one to keep them apart."

Ric had come into the kitchen to get a glass of lemonade. When he realized what they were talking about, he took his time so he could hear Mrs. Sanchez.

"It happened one night at the end of May, right at the end of the school year," Mrs. Sanchez began. "The weather was warm, and everyone had their windows open. I was sitting in my living room watching TV when I heard them start up again next door. Carlos was yelling, 'No,

you won't! You will not, Tony Robles!' and
Tony was shouting, 'But you don't understand! You're just a stupid old man who
doesn't understand anything!'

"I got up to close my window. The next
thing I knew I heard a lot of bumping and
thumping, like someone falling down
stairs. Then nothing. I waited a few minutes to see if they'd start yelling again, but
the house was quiet—dead quiet." Mrs.
Sanchez shuddered at the memory. "Oh,
I'll tell you, Louise, the silence was almost
worse than the fights. After that night, I
never saw Tony Robles again."

"Did you call the police, Mrs. Sanchez?"
Louise Salas had asked.

"No, and I'll tell you why. I had a friend
who was a secretary at Pierce High. She
told me that a couple of days later, Carlos
Robles called the school and said that
Tony had gone to visit relatives and would
not attend graduation services. The
school could do nothing about it. They
simply mailed Tony his diploma.

"That summer I didn't see Carlos at all.
Sometimes at night I would see light
around the edges of the curtains, so I

knew he was in there, but he always kept the shades drawn. Then one night toward the end of the summer..." Mrs. Sanchez looked down and closed her eyes. Ric waited for her to go on, but the old woman was quiet. Finally he could stand it no longer. He had to hear more.

"What, Mrs. Sanchez? What happened?" he demanded to know. The older woman turned and looked at him in surprise, as if she had forgotten he was there.

"Oh, my dear," Mrs. Sanchez whispered, shaking her head. "I saw Tony's ghost!"

"Where?" Ric had asked, sitting down at the table.

"In the attic of the Robles' house!"

"Tony's ghost?" Ric's mother had asked dubiously.

Mrs. Sanchez nodded her head. "Yes, I swear it. I was just going to bed when I heard a moaning sound. It came from the Robles' house. I went to my window and listened. From my bedroom, I can look up and see their attic window.

"I heard the moaning again. It was definitely coming from their attic. The shade was pulled, but the light inside the room threw shadows onto the shade. Suddenly I saw a silhouette—two silhouettes, actually. One was Carlos Robles. It looked as if he was sitting down. And the other was Tony—Tony Robles' ghost standing over his father!"

"But how could you be sure it was Tony?" Mrs. Salas had asked.

"Oh, it was him all right," the older woman said, nodding her head. "Tony had a very athletic build—very muscular and broad. And he had a certain way of holding his shoulders, straight as a soldier. It was definitely him."

"What happened then?" Ric wanted to know.

"The moaning grew louder. Then I saw Tony raise his hands into the air as if he was confused or upset." She paused.

"Go on," said Ric.

"Next thing I knew, Tony was bending down over his father. And the moaning stopped, just like that."

Both Ric and his mother looked confused. "What did Tony do?" Ric asked.

Mrs. Sanchez hesitated. "I know you probably won't believe this," she said, leaning closer to Ric and his mother, "but it looked as if he *kissed* his father on the forehead."

"Kissed him?" Ric had asked in surprise. "Why would a ghost do that?"

"Who knows? I'm only telling you what I saw. Perhaps to make amends. Tony probably died carrying as much guilt as his father had. Maybe he was trying to show his father that he was sorry for all the fighting they had done over the years."

"Oh, but, Mrs. Sanchez, there has to be a logical explanation for this," said Ric's mother. "Are you sure it couldn't have been someone else in the attic that night?"

"No, Louise. I'm sure it was Tony," Mrs. Sanchez said. "Mark my words, Tony Robles is dead. The fall down the stairs killed him. And his ghost still haunts his father's house!"

"But how was Tony's disappearance ever explained?" Ric had asked the older woman. "When he didn't come back to school in the fall, I mean."

"Believe it or not, it was Carlos himself who called the police—right after school started. I was outside working in my yard

when the police pulled up. I got a glimpse
of Robles when he came to the door to let
them in. How he had changed! He had
grown a grimy beard, and he had that
awful hat pulled down over his face. He
told them that Tony had not been with relatives that summer after all—that he had
made up that story because he didn't want
the school to know what had really happened. Then he told them about the fight
and how he had accidentally pushed Tony
down the stairs. He claimed that Tony,
bloody and raging, had run away afterward. Robles said that he had been waiting all summer for his son to return."

"Didn't the police investigate?" asked
Ric.

"Oh, yes, of course they did," Mrs.
Sanchez nodded her head. "They searched
the house and questioned some of the
neighbors. I told them exactly what I had
heard that night. But they never found a
body. And how do you look for one boy in
a country this size?"

Ric had to agree. It seemed like an
impossible task.

"Oh, they ran all the usual searches for

a missing person," the older woman continued, "but nothing turned up. No, he's dead. Believe me, Tony Robles is dead."

Mrs. Sanchez's words echoed in Ric's head as he stood looking out the window. He had been only twelve back then and had partly believed her story. Just like Eva and Peter, he had wanted to believe in ghosts. But he'd long since dismissed her claims as the imaginings of a superstitious woman who had too much time on her hands.

Now Ric watched Robles kneeling on the ground before the rosebush. In the moonlight, something gleamed in the grass at the old man's knees. What is that? Ric wondered, squinting his eyes. It looked like some kind of flat stone. Why hadn't he noticed it before? He'd lost his football near that rosebush a dozen times. Of course, each time Robles had chased him off immediately, so he never really had a chance to notice anything. Maybe the recent heavy rains had washed the dirt off the stone.

He watched as the old man picked a rose off the bush and laid it on the stone.

Suddenly, Ric realized what it was. A gravestone! That's Tony's grave, Ric thought, with a sense of shock and horror. The boy had died that night when his father pushed him down the stairs. And he was buried under the rosebush!

3 OVER THE YEARS, Ric had developed a strong dislike for the quiet, angry man who lived next door. Now he felt loathing. How could a father kill his son and then bury him in the backyard!

He watched Robles get up, spread some leaves and grass over the headstone, and head toward his house. Ric was about to leave the window when the old man stopped. His hat tipped back as he turned and looked up. Ric drew a sharp breath when their eyes met. For a long moment, Robles stared at Ric. Ric wanted to look away but couldn't. Robles' eyes seemed to be holding him, warning him. Finally, the old man turned away again and walked into his house.

Ric shivered. He heard a noise behind him and turned to see his mother standing in the doorway. "I saw your light, honey. What's wrong?"

Ric smiled at his mother. She was thirty-eight years old, but she could almost have passed for a teenager. Louise Salas had an inner beauty and a youthful nature. Ric loved his mother. She would never be so heartless as to hope that Ric would lose his chance to play football.

"I'm fine, Mom," Ric said. "I've been studying."

Mrs. Salas raised her eyebrows in surprise, then asked, "What were you looking at out the window?"

"Old man Robles. It's kind of weird. He was kneeling by his rosebush, and he was crying."

"*Mr.* Robles, Ric," his mother corrected. "Poor man. He must carry a lot of guilt over what happened to his son. Just think how he's suffered all these years, not knowing whether Tony is alive or dead."

"Uh…I think he knows, Mom."

"What do you mean?"

"I saw something that really freaked me tonight," Ric continued. "When old man, I mean, Mr. Robles was kneeling in front of the rosebush, I saw this flat stone on the ground in front of him. It looked like a gravestone or something. I think Tony is buried in that backyard!"

Mrs. Salas' large, dark eyes widened in disbelief. "Oh, Ricky! Don't be ridiculous!"

"But Mom, you know how they say Tony was never found—that he just disappeared that night," Ric said.

"But I don't think it's a gravestone, Ric. Maybe it's just a memorial to Tony that his father put there when he planted the rose-bush."

"But, Mom, maybe Tony *didn't* run away." Then he remembered the weird moaning sound he had heard and added quietly, "Maybe Mr. Robles did kill him, and Mrs. Sanchez's stories about seeing his ghost are true."

"Oh, Ric, you know that's ridiculous."

Ric shrugged his shoulders, slightly embarrassed. "I know, Mom."

"Señora Sanchez is a lonely, old woman who sometimes gets her memory mixed up with her imagination," Mrs. Salas continued. "She needs things to make her life interesting. You remember what a wild, reckless boy Tony was supposed to have been. Everyone in the neighborhood says so. It would have been just like him to run away."

"Maybe," said Ric. "But I'd sure like to know the truth about what happened that night."

"Ric, who knows what the truth is for sure? Don't spread this nonsense around about Tony being buried under the rose-bush. It would only cause trouble for Mr. Robles. And heaven knows, he has enough troubles already."

"I won't, Mom," Ric said. "But I'm going to keep an eye on him. Maybe I can find out what really happened that night."

* * *

In American history on Wednesday morning, Ric sat at his desk, sick to his stomach with fear. He'd tried to study, but he still wasn't sure he'd focused on the right things. Pike would probably stick in some trick questions to mess everybody up.

Before class began, Claudia leaned over to Ric. "I just know I'm gonna blow this test, and then I'll be tossed off the cheer squad. If I do, I'll die! Oh, I hate this guy so much!"

"Did you study?" Ric asked.

"Oh, right! Who can study for Pike's

tests? They're impossible," Claudia groaned. "He's out to get us, Ric."

Ric glanced over at Rafe and Stan. The two were sitting sullenly at their desks. When Mr. Pike came into the room, they glared at him with all the anger of an animal caught in a trap.

Mr. Pike pulled the tests from his briefcase. He always made several versions of his tests so students couldn't copy from others around them. He also kept a vigilant watch during his tests. A whisper from one student to another could mean an automatic F for both involved. That's why Ric couldn't imagine going to the principal and claiming that Pike allowed cheating to go on in his classes. The idea was ludicrous.

Ric received his test with shaky hands. Usually one look at Pike's tests made Ric give up any attempt at answering the questions. But this time, to his surprise, the material on the test looked familiar. Most of the multiple choice questions covered the parts of the chapter Ric had taken notes on. He found himself breezing through them.

"Wow, my studying really paid off," he thought to himself. Old Andy Jackson seemed almost as familiar to Ric as his own Uncle Eduardo.

Ric held his breath as he turned to the essay section. Mr. Pike's tests normally contained only one essay question worth fifty points. Ric read the question: "Evaluate the presidency of Andrew Jackson. Give specific examples of his successes and failures."

"Yeah!" Ric whispered, breathing a sigh of relief. He began writing quickly. He wrote about Jackson's foreign policy and about his fight against the Bank of the United States. He even remembered a quote from the textbook—"Jackson was a man of the people who carried out the people's will as a President should."

Ric was perspiring by the end of the test, but he felt good about it. For the first time ever, he figured he'd passed one of Pike's tests! He handed it in right before the bell rang.

As the students filed out, Stan muttered, "Man, he ambushed us! That creep made us think the test would be on the

War of 1812. Then he springs Jackson's presidency on us!"

"He did that on purpose," Claudia complained.

Ric distinctly remembered Mr. Pike saying the test would be on the last half of chapter four—Jackson's presidency. But he kept his mouth shut. He felt too good to get in an argument.

"We gotta dump this guy," Rafe seethed. "Let's meet in the courtyard today at lunch, okay? Then we can decide what to do."

Claudia narrowed her eyes and smiled. "I wouldn't miss it," she said.

Ric looked at Rafe and Stan, his teammates on the football team. They probably weren't the most desirable friends. In fact, Ric's father had often expressed his disapproval of them. Stan kept his head shaved and had a reputation for being a smart aleck in class. He drove a lime-green Camaro with a stereo system that could rock a neighborhood—a stereo on wheels, as Ric's dad called it. And then there was Rafe with his long black hair and trench coat from the Army surplus store. He looked like the bad guy in a Rambo movie. He was still on school probation for the fight he'd been in the year before. The only reason he was allowed to play football was because his social worker thought it would keep him out of trouble. But Ric had known these guys since seventh grade, and they had one important thing in common—they all loved playing football.

Then he looked at Claudia, a tall, strong girl with high cheekbones and a pair of lively brown eyes—his girl.

How could Ric turn against these people? Just because he felt he'd done well on the test, he couldn't ignore his friends. He didn't want to see Stan and Rafe kicked off the Panthers and Claudia deprived of her beloved cheerleading. She was the heart and spirit of the whole squad. She worked out with weights just so she could lift the other girls to her shoulders for the difficult gymnastic cheers.

"Yeah, okay, I'll be there," Ric mumbled. If nothing else, maybe I can talk some sense into them, he thought.

At lunch time, they gathered on the grass beside the weather-beaten statue of Franklin Pierce, the fourteenth president of the United States.

"Here's the deal," Rafe said. "One of us has got to go to the principal and tell him how everybody cheats in Pike's class while Pike sits at his desk reading trashy novels. Then we all have to back the story up."

Julie, Stan's girlfriend, laughed. "Oh, that's good. I like that!"

"How about you, Salas?" Rafe asked. "You wanna do it?"

"I don't think I could pull it off," Ric said, shaking his head. "I'm a lousy liar."

Rafe looked surprised and slightly angry. "You chickening out, man?" he demanded. "You're the logical one to do it. I've been suspended once already, so I don't think the principal would be too anxious to see me."

Julie giggled, "And I'm in detention constantly."

Stan had pointed out that he didn't have the best reputation either. "I don't think Mr. Kirn would even believe me," he said.

Finally Claudia shrugged and said, "Okay, you guys, I'll do it. I've got a clean record. I've probably got more of a reason to do it than any of you, anyway. I've got Pike for two classes—American history and publications. My life will be a lot easier if he's out of here!"

"Good girl, Claudia," Stan said, standing up. "You oughta be proud of your girl, Ric. She's got more guts than you!"

Ric and Claudia went to the Pizza Zone after football and cheerleading practice.

"You sure you want to go see the principal, Claudia?" Ric asked her. "About Pike, I mean."

Claudia held a big slice of pepperoni pizza to her lips. "Why not?" she said, taking a bite. "Nobody else wants the job!"

"But don't you think it's…um…you know, wrong?" Ric forced the words out.

"Wrong?" Claudia almost choked on her pizza. "It's wrong for him to make our lives miserable!"

"Yeah, but two wrongs don't make a right," Ric said, astonished that he was quoting his father.

Claudia made a face and wiped pizza

sauce off her lip. "Don't pull that right and wrong stuff on me, Ric. All I know is Pike's going to get me dumped off the cheer squad. If we could get somebody like Stephens from last year, we'd all be getting good grades."

"I guess you're right," said Ric.

Ric took Claudia home and then headed home himself. As he turned onto Linden Street, he saw Mr. Robles pulling his rusty old truck into his driveway. Ric noticed that even while he drove, he kept his hat pulled down over most of his face.

As he pulled into his own driveway, Ric felt Tony's medallion, still on the chain around his neck. He figured old Robles would be plenty burned up if he knew about *that*.

4
ALL NIGHT RIC thought about what they planned to do to Mr. Pike. He remembered seeing an old movie about a man who worked at an airplane factory that had government contracts to make military planes. Some of the men at the factory plotted to fix the books and cheat the government. The main character refused to go along with their plan and ended up losing his job and his so-called friends. After that, his family spiraled into debt. They almost lost their home. The man and his wife had to work two jobs each just to make ends meet. For a long time, the family practically lived on oatmeal and beans.

"But it was worth it," the main character had said to his son at the end of the movie. The family had stayed together, and the dishonest workers' plan had been exposed. "Now I can look at myself in the mirror and not feel ashamed. I still own my soul, understand?"

Ric thought about his own decision to go along with his friends' plans. If he did, who would own *his* soul?

When Ric arrived at school the next morning, he looked for Claudia. The five friends had agreed that after Claudia met with the principal, they would all back up her story if they were asked to.

Ric caught Claudia heading into algebra, her first class. "Claudia, I gotta tell you something before you talk to the principal about Pike," Ric said in a low voice. "I'm not sure I can be a part of that."

"What?" Claudia almost screamed. She ignored the stares from the students passing by.

"Mr. Pike doesn't let *anybody* cheat. Everybody knows that. I don't think I can back up a lie," Ric said.

Claudia's dark eyes flashed. "Well, I'm going ahead with our plans," she declared. "And if you stab us in the back, Ric Salas, you and me are through!" She spun around and went into algebra class, her shoulders stiff with anger.

Ric headed for English, shaking his head sadly. He hoped Claudia would have second thoughts about talking to the principal. He didn't want to lose her, but he just wasn't sure he could lie for her.

In history class third period, Mr. Pike returned the tests. Ric figured that Claudia, Stan, and Rafe all got F's because they were whispering bitterly to each other and glaring at the teacher. Rafe was clenching and unclenching his fists over and over. Ric was nervous about his own grade now. Maybe he'd been overly confident. Maybe he'd failed too.

Mr. Pike slapped the test face down on Ric's desk and moved on to the next student. Ric forced himself to turn the paper over and look at the grade. Then he gasped. An A-minus! And scrawled in red at the top of the page was the single word "Bravo!"

Wow! Wait until Dad sees this! Ric thought.

Claudia glanced over. "You rat!" she hissed. "No wonder you're having second thoughts. Just because you did okay, you don't care about the rest of us. Some friend you are!"

When the students filed out at the end

of the period, Ric found himself walking next to Tina Lanza. Tina glanced down at the test sticking out of Ric's history book.

"Good goin', Ric," she said. "I only got a B-plus!"

"Thanks, Tina," Ric said. "I guess I got lucky."

"There's no such thing as luck in this class," Tina said. "You either know it or you don't."

"I guess," admitted Ric.

"You must be a lot smarter than you let on, Ric," said Tina. Then she smiled. "Who says jocks are dumb, anyway?" She headed out the door and down the hall.

Ric laughed. He liked Tina. He hadn't realized before how nice she was.

Outside the classroom, Claudia, Stan, and Rafe were standing in a group. As Ric approached, Claudia gave him a cold look. "I talked to the principal during second period. I had study hall," Claudia was saying to the others. "I'm not sure he believed me, but he said he'd look into it."

"All right!" Rafe cried, giving Claudia a high-five. "This is only the beginning. We'll nail that little weasel good!"

Ric said nothing. Maybe the principal wouldn't ask him about cheating in Pike's class. Maybe he'd never have to make the choice between telling the truth or keeping his friends.

After school, Ric headed for practice. As he crossed the campus, Vic Compton, the football coach, hailed him. "Hey, Ric, how are you doing with your grades? You okay for the big game tomorrow night?" The Panthers were playing Wilson this week. For the last two years, the Panthers had humiliated the other team, and now the Wolverines were out for revenge.

"I'm okay," Ric said. "I'm sure I brought my grade up in the class I was worried about."

"That's great," the coach said. "Now go get suited up for practice."

But just then, to Ric's disappointment, Mr. Kirn, the principal came along. "Ric… would you come into my office for a few minutes?" he asked.

Once inside the office, Ric sat fidgeting as Mr. Kirn asked, "You're in Mr. Pike's American history class, aren't you?"

"Yes," Ric said.

"Have you ever noticed anything out of the ordinary going on in that class?" Mr. Kirn asked.

"What do you mean?" asked Ric.

Mr. Kirn continued. "I've had a complaint today that cheating is widespread during tests in that class. I just talked with Mr. Pike a few minutes ago. I told him I'd be checking into this matter. Now, Ric, have you ever seen cheating going on in Mr. Pike's class?"

Ric bit his lip and looked at the floor.

"I'd appreciate an honest answer from you, Ric. And don't worry. Everything you say will be kept confidential."

Ric shifted in his chair. He coughed a few times, cleared his throat, and then said, "I've never seen any cheating in that class, Mr. Kirn."

"Have you heard any other students complaining about cheating going on in that class?" Mr. Kirn asked.

"No," Ric mumbled.

Mr. Kirn pressed on. "In your opinion then, Ric, does cheating take place in Mr. Pike's American history class?"

Ric looked at the principal. "You're sure

this is confidential?"

"Of course, Ric."

Ric took a deep breath. "Then, no, sir, in my opinion, there's no cheating in Mr. Pike's class."

"Thank you, Ric," Mr. Kirn said, standing up and opening the door. "That will be all."

Ric hoped he could sneak away from the principal's office without being seen. He also hoped a lot of other students would be questioned by Mr. Kirn. He knew the good students would tell the truth, that Pike's class was on the up-and-up. Maybe that would put an end to it, and his friends would never have to know that he'd let them down.

When Ric suited up for practice, he noticed that Stan and Rafe weren't there. As he ran onto the field, he saw them standing in front of the bleachers. They headed his way.

"Why aren't you suited up?" Ric asked his friends, although he was afraid he already knew the answer.

"We got bumped because of Pike's stinkin' test," Rafe snarled.

"Hey, man, I'm sorry," Ric said.

"We're gonna get Pike. I swear it, man," Stan said angrily. "I already talked to the principal. I backed up Claudia's story all the way. How about you? He talked to you yet?"

Ric's mind spun. "Uh...yeah. He just nabbed me a little while ago. He...like asked a few general questions. I said, yeah, guys cheated and stuff like that," Ric lied.

"All right!" Stan said with a grin.

The cheerleaders were practicing on the other end of the field. Ric looked for Claudia and saw her standing on the sidelines.

"Oh, no," said Ric. "Looks like Claudia got the ax too."

Claudia walked over to them despondently. She had tears in her eyes, and her hands were clenched.

"I'm off the cheer squad until my history grade is up," she cried. "That filthy little creep Pike! I hate him so much!"

"I'm sorry, Claudia," Ric said.

Claudia glowered at Ric. "You said you might not back up what I told the principal. So did you or not?"

Stan looked shocked, "Hey, man, what's she saying?"

"Uh…I sorta had second thoughts about lying about Pike. You know, man, I've never done anything like that."

"Yeah? And?" asked Rafe, his eyes narrowing.

"But then I did the right thing," Ric said quickly. He felt his face getting warm. "I told the principal that everybody cheats in Pike's class." He could see relief on the faces of his friends.

"Good. Just so you did," Claudia said. She lowered her voice. "We gotta stick together on this. If they find out I lied, I'll never be on the cheer squad again, even if I get straight A's."

Claudia went to join her friends on the squad again. They had stopped practicing and were huddled around her, lamenting over her misfortune.

"Hey, I gotta go, man," Stan said. "I told Julie I'd take her to work—now that I don't have *practice!* Later, you guys."

"Later," said Ric.

Ric was alone with Rafe. His friend had

a look in his eyes that Ric had never seen before.

"So you told Claudia you wouldn't lie about Pike…" Rafe began.

"Well, like I said…I chickened out—but just for a minute."

Rafe lay a beefy hand on Ric's arm. He outweighed Ric by at least twenty-five pounds. Ric knew Rafe could be a mean fighter if he got riled.

"Ric, my man, we're all in this together, right?"

Ric nodded.

"And we gotta trust each other, right?" Rafe continued, squeezing Ric's arm slightly. "I mean, if we're gonna destroy Pike, then we gotta do it as a team. Otherwise it's not gonna work. And we don't want any traitors on the team. Am I right?"

"Yeah, you're right," Ric said. He could feel his mouth going dry.

"Now, I'd like to believe that you backed up Claudia with the principal. But I gotta put two and two together. You're not off the team. And you passed that last test. You're in the clear, man. So why would you care what happens to the rest of us?"

"Hey, you're my friends, man," Ric stammered.

"Well, I'd like you to prove that, Ric." Rafe reached into his pocket and brought out a big silver key, which he dropped into Ric's hand.

"What's this for?" Ric asked.

Rafe placed his arm around Ric's shoulders, turning him slightly. "You see the teachers' parking lot over there?" he asked.

Ric nodded.

"And see Pike's red Beemer? It's an old one, but he keeps it all shiny and nice. I bet it'd break his little heart if he got a nasty old scratch down the side of it."

Ric swallowed hard. He knew what was coming.

"So go do it, man," Rafe said. "Prove you're on our side and not his."

Perspiration popped out on Ric's skin. This was his chance to prove himself. If he did this, no one would suspect that he hadn't backed up Claudia's story. The key in his hand felt like a burning coal.

5 RIC STOOD FOR a long moment and stared at the key. Then he shook his head slowly and looked at Rafe. "No, man. I'm not gonna do it."

Rafe glared at Ric. "You liar!" he hissed. "You backed Pike when you talked to the principal, didn't you?"

"What if I did?" Ric shot back. "I'm not lying for you or anybody!" Ric threw down the key, turned sharply, and ran to join the other players on the field.

Ric's dad was working in the garage when Ric came home after practice.

"Hi, Ric," Mr. Salas said.

"What're you doin', Pop?" Ric asked.

"Tuning up the lawn mower. It's been running kind of rough lately." Ric watched for a few minutes as his father removed the old spark plugs and replaced them with new ones.

"So, how are you doing in American history?" Mr. Salas asked, without looking up from his work.

Ric was waiting for this question.

"Well...I got my chapter test back today..." he began hesitantly.

"And?" his father turned and looked at him.

"I passed! I got an A-minus!"

"*Ay!* I knew you could do it, son! An A-minus!" his father cried, clapping Ric on the back.

"And I didn't lose my eligibility either," Ric said. "Now I can keep playing football." Ric watched his father for a reaction.

"Well, I'd say you deserve the chance to play, son," his father said. "And your mother and I will be there to watch you!"

"All right! Thanks, Pop!"

It was a warm evening, so Ric shot some baskets with Peter before dinner. Peter was tall for his age and was already a pretty good player.

"Basketball's gonna be your game, Peter," Ric said.

"Yeah, but I'm gonna play football too, Ric. Just like you!" Peter said with open admiration.

Just then a car rumbled down the street, riding low and slow. Ric recognized it as Stan's lime-green Camaro. Claudia was in the car, along with Julie and Rafe. The Camaro slowed down in front of Ric's house, and Rafe leaned out.

"Hey, kid!" he yelled at Peter. "Your brother is a slimebag who deserts his friends!"

"Leave Peter out of this," Ric shouted back.

Rafe ignored Ric. "The Panthers are gonna lose tomorrow, Peter, 'cause your brother turned his back on all his friends," he yelled.

Stan hammered on his horn, blasting the neighborhood with a loud din. Then he turned up some rap music to top volume, and the very asphalt on the street seemed to vibrate as the car sped away.

"What was he talking about, Ric?" Peter asked in a strained voice.

Ric put his hand on his brother's shoulder. "Nothing, *hermano*. He's just a creep."

"But how come your friends are mad at you?" Peter asked. "I saw Claudia in the car too."

"They wanted me to lie about something, and I wouldn't do it," Ric said. "So now they hate me."

"Do you think the Panthers are gonna lose Friday like they said?" Peter asked.

"No way, little brother." Ric put his arm around Peter's shoulders. "Because guys like me are gonna play extra hard to make sure we win."

Peter grinned. "All right!" he said.

As Ric got ready for school the next morning, he thought about Mr. Pike. How did he feel about the allegations against him? Did he know which students made them? How would Mr. Pike act in class that day? But Ric never got a chance to find out. The pep rally for the big game that evening took place during third period.

As the cheerleaders attempted to lead the students in a rousing chant, Ric couldn't help noticing that Claudia was absent from the squad. One of the subs had taken her place.

Ric spotted Claudia sitting with Rafe a few rows down. Once she turned her head slightly, and Ric could see the tears gleaming in her eyes. He felt a pang of guilt as he remembered his part in her situation.

But then he looked over to where the faculty stood. While most of the other teachers joined in the cheer, Mr. Pike was leaning back against the wall with his arms folded and a dejected look on his face. Dad was right, Ric thought. Two wrongs *don't* make a right.

* * *

The mood was tense as the Panthers put on their gear Friday evening. Stan and Rafe had done a good job of spreading it around that Ric was a traitor to the team. Some of the guys, like Ben Gibson, the quarterback, were sympathetic to Ric. But most of the guys, especially the ones in Mr. Pike's class, resented him. Stan and Rafe were both popular team players. They had often made the difference in close games.

"You *and* Pike are gonna be sorry if we lose this game," Joel Adams, a big linebacker, threatened Ric as they suited up.

In the locker room, Coach Compton spoke to the team. "I don't have to tell you that we're hurting because we lost two key players," he said. "It's too bad.

Wilson's tougher than ever this year, and we could have used them tonight."

Some of the players grumbled. Others glared at Ric.

"But let me tell you this," the coach continued, shaking his finger. "Any player who doesn't keep his grades up is off the team—no questions asked by me or anyone else! It's school policy, and we have to abide by it whether we like it or not. Is that clear?"

"Yeah, Coach," a few of the players said half-heartedly.

Next the coach reviewed some of the plays they had been working on that week.

"Any questions?" he asked when he was finished. There were none.

"Good. Now, like I said, we're short two players, so I don't expect one hundred percent from you guys. I expect one hundred and *fifty* percent. Now go out there and play the game of your lives!"

As they ran onto the field, Ric looked over at the other team's bench. He agreed with Coach—the Wolverines looked tougher and meaner than they'd ever looked before.

Then he glanced at the cheerleaders. They were having a hard time firing up the crowd. It was obvious that Claudia was sorely missed. She screamed louder, jumped higher, and showed more wild enthusiasm than any of the other girls. Ric glanced around for Claudia in the stands but didn't see her.

Just before the teams took the field, somebody delivered a note to Ric. He immediately recognized Claudia's handwriting.

"I hope you lose, Ric Salas. It would serve you right for what you did to me!"

Ric shuddered at the angry tone of the note. How quickly Claudia had changed from being his girl to being his enemy. As he bunched up the note and tossed it away, he glanced up into Wilson's bleachers. Sitting in the middle of the Wolverines' stands were Claudia, Stan, Julie, and Rafe. They were surrounded by a lot of their friends.

The two teams took the field. With the game underway for three minutes, the Panthers had possession of the ball, and Gibson threw a pass to Ric. Ric had the ball in his fingertips but fumbled it away. The Wolverines recovered. A loud cheer went up from the Wilson stands. Ric glanced up and saw Claudia's hateful grin. She was holding up a handpainted sign that read "Drop dead, Ric."

6 THE WOLVERINES SCORED a touchdown, and cheers exploded from their stands. It was going just like Claudia and the others had hoped. Ric knew that everyone would remember who had fumbled the ball and given the Wolverines their momentum.

Ric reached up and touched Tony's medallion. Maybe some of Tony's magic on the field was still in the medal. Ric didn't really believe that, but he rubbed the medallion anyway. And he said under his breath, "Hey, Tony, give me some help! Please!"

The Wolverines were heading toward the end zone again, and the replacement players for Stan and Rafe missed some key blocks. Another Wolverine touchdown sent the Wilson stands into an uproar. Ric could imagine Claudia and her group cheering right along with them.

After the kickoff, Ric caught a pass. This time he took a firm hold on the ball and tore seventy yards into the end zone, scoring a Panther touchdown. Last week the Panthers' stands would have exploded with cheers. But this week Ric's play was met with only a tepid response from the Pierce fans.

In the second half, the two teams each scored a touchdown. Ric caught two more passes. In the final minutes, the Panthers made the last touchdown and soared to victory. Ric slapped hands and exchanged high-fives with Ben and Coach Compton.

"You came through like a champ," Coach Compton said, slapping Ric on the back.

In the locker room, Ric took off his gear and showered, then put on a pair of jeans and a pullover. Usually after the game, the team and their supporters would head for the Pizza Zone. Ric normally took several kids in his car. But this time, Ric walked to his car alone. He knew that the gang had gone ahead without him.

What a night this might have been, he thought sadly. The first time ever that Ric Salas had won a game almost single-handedly! Oh, well, he thought, there's always little Peter. He's probably home by now and just waiting for a chance to discuss the game with me.

As Ric unlocked his car door, a familiar voice said, "Good game, Ric."

Ric turned to see Mr. Pike approaching.

"Oh, hi, Mr. Pike," Ric said, surprised that the teacher had come to the game after what had happened. "I…um…didn't expect to see you here tonight."

"Well, I have to admit that I had some reservations about coming." He paused, then continued. "You know about the lies about me, don't you, Ric?"

"Yeah," Ric said, not wanting to admit just how *much* he knew about it.

Mr. Pike nodded and leaned back against Ric's car. "I figured you'd heard about it through the grapevine by now. It really bothered me at first. But then I told myself that any claim that I allow cheating in class is ridiculous. Everyone knows that." He paused again, as if he was anticipating a remark from Ric.

"Um, right. Everybody knows that," Ric said.

"Anyway, I have faith that the good students will tell the truth, and I can put this thing behind me." This time he looked directly into Ric's eyes.

"I hope so, Mr. Pike," Ric said.

"You know, Ric, you really were outstanding tonight," Mr. Pike continued. "I'd say that was one for the records."

"Thanks, Mr. Pike."

"And speaking of records," said Mr. Pike. "You know I'm advisor of the school paper?"

Ric nodded.

"Well, the journalism students have asked me if they can put out a special edition. They'd like to pay a tribute to all the athletes over the years who have set school records. You know, like the longest broad jump or the most touchdowns in a game."

"Sounds great," said Ric. "I'd like to read it when it comes out."

"The kids mentioned a football player from about ten years ago—a Tony Robles. He was supposed to have set the record for the most touchdowns scored in a championship game—three, I think."

"Four," Ric corrected him.

"Anyway, I guess he disappeared or something?"

"Yeah...that's the story, anyway," Ric said, remembering the gravestone under the rosebush in the Robles' yard.

"Well, I'd like to talk to his family and get some quotes for the article on him. I didn't want to send any of the students because I hear Mr. Robles is a pretty crusty old fellow. But one of the kids said the Robles' house is next to yours—on Linden Street, right?"

Ric nodded.

"Do you think Mr. Robles would talk to me?" the teacher asked.

"I don't think so, Mr. Pike. I wouldn't mess with him," Ric warned.

"Well, I wanted to give him the opportunity to be part of the tribute to his son. That's what we're doing with the other families. And Tony was a legendary running back. It sounds like he might have gone pro had things turned out differently."

Ric shook his head. "Robles won't even talk to his neighbors. I'm telling you, Mr. Pike, the man isn't playing with a full deck. You'd better just stay away from that guy."

Ric was tempted to say more but didn't. He remembered his mother asking him not to tell anyone about his suspicions.

"Well, I'll give it a shot anyway. I thought I'd stop over there on my way home. What can it hurt? The worst he can do is slam the door in my face, right?"

"Uh…right," Ric said. He realized he'd better leave before he said more. "Well, I gotta go. I'll see you Monday, Mr. Pike."

"Okay, Ric," the teacher said. "See you Monday." He headed off across the parking lot.

Ric took the long way home. He didn't want to be around when Mr. Pike pulled up next door. Pike might see him and ask Ric to accompany him to the Robles' house.

He slowed down as he passed the Pizza Zone. Bright lights shone through the windows of the little restaurant. He could imagine the fun the kids from Pierce were having in there. Any other night he would have been celebrating with them.

Suddenly he felt lonely. Maybe he

should have gone along with Claudia and Stan in their efforts to oust Pike. Sure, he'd managed to "keep his soul" by telling the truth, but what good did it do him if he lost his friends in the process?

Still concerned about running into Mr. Pike, Ric decided to park his car in the alley behind his house. Then he could avoid pulling into the driveway from Linden Street.

The alley was dark, and Ric drove slowly. He knew that cats often invaded the garbage cans in the alley at night. He didn't want to hit one as it tried to escape his headlights.

Ric pulled up next to the back of his garage and put his car in park. As he reached for the keys to turn off the car, he stopped. In the light of his headlights, he saw something move further down the alley. At first he thought it was a prowling cat, but then he realized it was a person.

Ric scrambled out of his car, leaving the headlights on. He ran down the alley, his shadow stretching out on the ground in front of him. A man lay face down on the gravel. As Ric approached, he saw the handle of a knife sticking out of the man's back. Blood streamed from the wound, soaking his white shirt and the gravel beneath him.

Ric fell to his knees. With trembling hands, he gently turned the man's face into the light.

"Mr. Pike!" he gasped.

7 RIC LEANED CLOSE to the injured man's face and listened. He's still breathing, he thought with relief. But I've got to get help.

He ran for home. As he burst into the kitchen, his mother looked up in surprise.

"Call 911!" Ric cried. "Mr. Pike's been stabbed! He's in the alley!" He ran back outside.

Ric returned to Mr. Pike's side. "Hold on, Mr. Pike," he whispered. "Just hold on."

When Ric looked up, he saw his parents hurrying through the backyard.

"Ric, are you all right?" his mother called anxiously as she approached.

"Yeah, Mom. I'm fine. But Mr. Pike..." Ric's voice cracked.

"It's all right, Ricky," his mother said. She covered the teacher with a blanket she had grabbed from home. "I called 911. We'll just wait with him until the ambulance comes."

Mr. Salas put his hand on Ric's shoulder. "What happened, son?"

"I don't know. I just pulled into the alley and saw him. There was no one else around."

"Well, that was quick thinking, Ric," Mr. Salas said. "You may have saved Mr. Pike's life." He shook his head. "Imagine, Louise—a mugger almost right behind our house."

Ric looked down at his teacher. I told you not to come, he thought. I told you old man Robles was crazy. If you'd have listened to me, this never would have happened. Then he noticed Mr. Pike's watch gleaming in the beams of the headlights.

"Look, his watch is still on his wrist!" Ric said. He thought he remembered seeing Mr. Pike's wallet sticking out of his back pocket.

Carefully he lifted the blanket and looked underneath. "And his wallet—he still has it!" He knew a mugger would have taken those valuables.

"Maybe you scared off the attacker," his father said, his eyes scanning the darkness.

Ric glanced at the Robles' house. A fresh theory came rushing into his brain. Old man Robles had seen the nicely dressed young man at his door. Robles never got visitors. He must have thought Mr. Pike was a police detective. After all, Robles had seen Ric watching him the other night. He probably thought Ric had reported seeing the gravestone under the rosebush. Robles assumed he was under arrest and panicked. After he let Mr. Pike in, he stabbed him, probably with one of those knives he used to gut fish. Then he dumped him in the alley.

Suddenly Ric was swept with guilt. He *should* have reported the grave in the backyard! Then this might not have happened.

"He wasn't mugged, Dad," he said finally. "He was attacked."

Before he could say more, the wail of sirens shattered the quiet neighborhood. Within minutes, police and paramedics swarmed the alley.

As the paramedics worked feverishly to stop the bleeding from the stab wound, Ric told an Officer Lynn Thomas about finding Mr. Pike. The officer asked Ric a few questions, took his name, address, and phone number, and went off to question people in the neighboring houses. She never asked Ric if he knew what Pike was doing in the neighborhood, and Ric didn't volunteer the information. Robles had warned him that night with his eyes—warned him to mind his own business. Ric was not going to risk ending up like Mr. Pike.

Ric watched sadly as the teacher was loaded into the ambulance.

"Come on, honey," Mrs. Salas said, putting her arm around his shoulders. "Turn your headlights off and lock up your car. There's nothing we can do now."

* * *

That night Eva came into Ric's room.

"How're you doing?" she wanted to know.

"Okay," Ric answered. He was lying on his bed looking up at the ceiling.

"Pretty scary, huh?" Eva asked, sitting on the edge of the bed. "I mean, about Mr. Pike being mugged."

"He wasn't mugged, Eva. He still had his watch and billfold on him," said Ric.

"So what do you think happened?" Eva asked.

Ric looked at his sister. "Eva, can you keep a secret?" he asked.

"Sure, you know I can, Ric," she answered.

"Are you sure? I mean, if I tell you this, you can't tell anyone. Understand?"

"My lips are sealed," said Eva.

"Okay. Last Sunday, I fell asleep reading my American history book. I woke up around midnight. It was storming outside real bad."

"Yeah, I remember Sunday," Eva said. Ric was about to go on when she added quietly, "I heard Tony's ghost that night."

"You heard it too? That's what I was going to tell you. At first I thought it was the wind, but when I listened closer, it really did sound like someone moaning. Why didn't you tell me you heard it?"

"Because you always laugh at me when I talk about Tony's ghost."

"Well, I'm still not sure it's a ghost, but at least now I know what you're talking about," Ric said.

Eva breathed a sigh of relief.

"But that's not all I was going to tell you," Ric continued. "A few nights later, I was up late again. Right before I went to bed, I looked out the window. I saw old man Robles out in his backyard." Ric went on to explain about the gravestone he had seen that night.

"A gravestone?" Eva cried. "What would a gravestone be doing in…" Her voice trailed off as she realized what Ric was implying.

"Let's just say I don't think there's any doubt where Tony is," Ric said.

"Oh, Ric, that's so horrible. We live next door to a cemetery—and a ghost!" Eva shuddered.

"Well, I still don't know about the ghost part, but I'm pretty sure that's Tony's grave."

"But, Ric, Tony should be buried in a real cemetery in blessed ground," Eva said.

"Yeah, he should. But remember, Eva, you said you wouldn't tell anyone about this."

"I know. I won't." She paused, then said, "So Robles really *did* kill Tony."

"It looks like it. And…um…you asked me what I think happened to Mr. Pike…"

Eva frowned, then gasped. "Ric, no! You think Robles stabbed him?"

"Well, that's where Mr. Pike was headed tonight—to talk to Robles about Tony's football days."

"But why would he hurt Mr. Pike?"

"Who knows what goes through that old man's head? I think he probably thought Mr. Pike was a detective snooping around."

"After all this time? But why?"

"Because he saw me watching him that night—the night I saw Tony's grave!"

Eva's eyes widened. "He did? Oh, my gosh, Ric. If Robles thinks you called the police on him, you could be in danger!"

"I know, Eva. That's why I didn't say anything to the police tonight. I'd like to know for sure first before I go accusing him—or I could end up like Mr. Pike!"

Eva shook her head. "And I thought you were going to tell me that Stan or Rafe or someone did it."

"Why would I think that?"

"Well, I saw them at the game tonight. I could tell they were really mad about not being allowed to play. Rafe especially. He looked like he was going to explode with anger. And he had this big knife. He was cleaning his fingernails with it or something."

"A knife? What kind of knife?" Ric asked.

"I don't know—just a big knife."

Ric hadn't considered Rafe or Stan before. After all, they were just kids. But he had played enough football with them to know how mean they could be. Especially Rafe. He actually enjoyed hurting other guys on the field. And the fight he was in last year—he busted another kid over the head with a bottle. But sticking a knife in Mr. Pike?

Over the weekend, Ric called Oceanside Community Hospital to check on Mr. Pike's condition. Since he wasn't a family member, he couldn't get much information. But he did learn that Mr. Pike was in intensive care.

At school on Monday morning, Ric met

Ben Gibson in the hall.

"Hey, man," Ben said. "I heard Mr Pike was knifed in the alley behind your house."

"Yeah," said Ric. "It was awful."

"So how's he doing?" Ben asked. "I mean, is he going to live or what?" Ric noticed that Ben seemed surprised, but not terribly upset.

"He's in critical condition," Ric said. "That's all I know."

Ben seemed to be considering that information. Then he said, "So I guess he won't be back teaching history, huh?"

"Not for a while anyway," Ric answered.

"You know," Ben said, "if we'd get an easy sub for Pike, the guys could get back their eligibility in time for the big games." He saw the shocked look on Ric's face. "Well, we can't always count on playing as well as we did the other night, you know."

As Ben walked away, Ric shook his head. He couldn't believe Ben was already trying to take advantage of the tragedy.

Ric walked into American history and saw a new teacher at the front of the room, busily trying to get organized for class. Then he saw Claudia by her desk doing high-fives with Stan and Rafe. It made him sick. He wondered how he could have ever liked such a girl.

Dennis Adams was a handsome young teacher fresh out of college. He didn't look much older than the seniors, and he was eager to please.

"Don't you guys be shy about telling me when I'm out of line," he said. "I expect to learn as much from you as you'll learn from me!"

Everybody laughed and nudged each other. Ric heard Claudia say, "This is gonna be like takin' candy from a baby!"

Great, Ric thought. Just what we need. A teacher who wants to be everybody's best friend.

"Furthermore, I won't bore you with a lot of details from some dull textbook," Adams went on. "We'll just discuss the issues in each chapter."

For the next forty minutes, Mr. Adams led, or tried to lead, a discussion on Manifest Destiny. Most of the class hadn't read the assignment. And the rest, like

Ric, didn't feel like discussing anything after what had happened to Mr. Pike.

The bell rang, and the students filed from the classroom. On the way out, Ric heard a lot of remarks about Mr. Adams.

"What a cool guy, and a hunk too!" a girl said.

"Passing this class will be a piece of cake now," one boy laughed.

Then Tina Lanza said, "You guys, we really should send Mr. Pike a get-well card."

"Let's send him a *don't*-get-well card instead," Stan suggested, laughing.

"No, let's send him a 'glad you're there and not here' card," Claudia giggled.

"You guys are sick," Ric said, disgusted.

Claudia looked at him coldly. "What's your problem?" she asked.

"Well, it's not funny," Ric continued. "Mr. Pike could be dying!"

"Pike is gone," Claudia said flatly, "and that's good. He was a lousy teacher. And he was unfair. Like my mom always says, what goes around comes around. At least *I'm* honest enough to admit that I'm glad he's gone!"

At lunch time, Ric made sure not to eat in his regular spot. He didn't want to risk being hassled by any of his former friends. Then again, he thought, now that Pike's gone, they might actually be friendly to me again. He wasn't sure which was worse.

But Claudia found him anyway—and she was friendly. In fact, she seemed downright cheerful. "Hey, Ric, wasn't that guy Adams great in history today?" she asked, sitting down.

"I guess," he said, taking a drink of milk.

Claudia noticed the abrupt answer. "Come on, Ric," she said. "Lighten up."

"A guy could be dying as we speak, and you want me to lighten up?" Ric asked.

Claudia put her hand over Ric's. "Mr. Pike'll be fine," she said. "Doctors can work wonders today. But think about it, Ric. Pike really wasn't good for Pierce— and he wouldn't have been good for you in the long run. He kept guys like Rafe and Stan off the football team. We got lucky Friday night, but eventually that would have hurt us. We're going to lose more games without those guys."

Ric shrugged.

"And you know not many college scouts come to check out guys on losing teams."

"Maybe," Ric said. He had to admit that Claudia had a point.

Claudia pressed on. "Look, Ric. I'm sorry about how I acted at the game last Friday. I was just so upset over being kicked off the squad. I mean, I've been a cheerleader since sixth grade! It's like my whole life. I take dance lessons so I can be a better cheerleader. I go to a camp for cheerleading every summer. I lift weights constantly. Don't you understand? If I don't cheer, I'm nothing."

"I know it means a lot to you, Claudia," Ric said.

"Adams is my big chance, Ric. If I can get my grade up, I can be head cheerleader in time for the really big games. Like when we play North or Lincoln. And with guys like Stan and Rafe back, we could make it to the championship, and I could be cheering in front of thousands. Somebody important could see me…" Claudia's eyes were shining with hope.

"So are we friends again, Ric?" she pleaded. "You're still a sweet guy and a fabulous football player...all that stood between us was Pike, and now he's gone."

"You talk as if he's dead," Ric said.

Claudia shrugged. "No, but he won't be back in time to wreck this semester." Then she gave him the look that used to make him melt. "Friends?" she asked sweetly.

Ric knew he'd never feel the same about Claudia again, but he didn't hate her. "Sure, friends," he said.

Stan and Rafe came over just as Ric stood up to leave. Stan was saying to Rafe, "Yeah, we got lucky with ol' Pike. Some mugger solved our problem for us. How about that? Who says crime doesn't pay?"

"It wasn't a mugger," Ric snapped. "Mr. Pike's wallet and watch were untouched. You tell me what mugger would leave those behind!"

"So what are you sayin', Ric?" Stan asked, narrowing his eyes.

"Yeah, who cares what happened as long as he's gone?" Rafe said.

"I just hope nobody from this school stuck a knife in him," Ric said.

Rafe came closer. "You accusin' somebody, Salas?"

"I didn't mention any names, man. But now that you bring it up, somebody saw you cleaning your nails with a mean-looking knife Friday night. You still got that knife?" Ric asked.

Ric was sure he saw a flash of surprise in Rafe's dark eyes. "I said, you still got the knife, man?" Ric repeated.

"I lost it," Rafe said. "I don't have it anymore!" With that he turned and stalked off, his long black ponytail streaming out behind him.

8 THAT EVENING, RIC went to the hospital. Mr. Pike was still in the intensive care unit, so he couldn't see him. In the visitors' lounge Ric saw Tina Lanza consoling a young woman. He knew it must be Mrs. Pike.

As he approached, Tina looked up and smiled a sad smile.

"Hi," she said quietly.

"Hi, Tina," Ric said. The young woman looked up. He could tell she had been crying.

"Mrs. Pike?" Ric said. "I'm Ric Salas, one of your husband's students. I know I can't see Mr. Pike, but I brought this card. Can I leave it with you?"

"Yes, of course," Mrs. Pike said, wiping her eyes. "I'm so glad you've come. It would mean so much to him to know that his students are here."

"How's Mr. Pike doing?" Ric asked.

"He's still in critical condition. But the doctors have given us some hope. They say if he can make it through the next twenty-four hours, he has a good chance. We're praying hard."

"Everyone is," Ric said.

On the way home, Ric stopped in to see Mrs. Sanchez.

"Ric, come in. Come in," she said smiling.

"Thanks, Mrs. Sanchez," Ric said.

"Have a seat." The older woman gestured toward a large green sofa. "Can I get you anything? A glass of iced tea, maybe?"

"No, thanks," said Ric. "I can't stay long. I just came over to talk to you about the other night—Friday night."

"Oh," said Mrs. Sanchez, her expression turning somber. "That was terrible, so terrible. I feel so sorry for that young man. How is he doing? Have you heard?"

"Yeah, I just came from the hospital. He's still in critical condition."

"Oh, dear," said Mrs. Sanchez. "I was afraid something terrible like this might happen someday." She glanced out her window toward the Robles' house.

"Mrs. Sanchez," Ric began. "Do you remember if Mr. Robles was around the night Mr. Pike was attacked? I mean, did the police question him or anything?"

"He was around," Mrs. Sanchez said. "I remember seeing him pull in with his truck earlier. But when the police came—poof! He was gone."

"Did you see anything that night?" Ric asked.

"No, I saw nothing. I was in bed asleep when it happened. The police woke me up when they pounded on my door. I thought the world had come to an end!"

"What did you mean when you said you were afraid something terrible would happen?" asked Ric.

Mrs. Sanchez looked down at her hands folded in her lap. "I know you think I'm just a silly old woman, Ric. Most of the neighbors do. But something strange has been going on in that house for years, ever since Tony disappeared. I'm home more than the other neighbors are. I hear things and see things that are not right over there."

"So what are you saying, Mrs. Sanchez?"

Mrs. Sanchez leaned forward toward

Ric and said in a low voice, "I am saying maybe the *aparecido* attacked Mr. Pike."

"The *aparecido?* The ghost?" Ric asked, remembering his Spanish.

"Yes, Ric. Tony's ghost. I think it roams around, full of rage and hate. I hear it— lately more than ever. I think it's been tormenting the old man for years. Perhaps the ghost is responsible for the attack on the teacher."

Ric didn't mention the moaning he had heard last week to Mrs. Sanchez. He thought it would only make her more afraid. He also didn't tell her about the gravestone in Robles' yard. But he made up his mind once and for all to check out that gravestone. Maybe there was something written on it that would prove that Tony Robles was dead. Then he could go to the police. They would arrest Robles for the murder of Tony, and Ric could tell them what he knew about Friday night.

"Mrs. Sanchez," Ric said, "has Mr. Robles been back since Friday night?"

"I don't think so. I haven't seen any lights on in the house since then. The police have been back twice that I know of, but Robles hasn't answered the door."

"Thanks, Mrs. Sanchez," Ric said, standing up. "I'd better be going now."

"You're welcome, Ric. You come any time. I get lonely in this big old house by myself. I always welcome company."

As Ric left, he made up his mind to visit Mrs. Sanchez more often. She was a nice lady, and no one should have to be lonely in a world with so many people, he thought.

Ric headed toward the Robles' house. The place gave him a creepy feeling. The yard was overgrown with weeds, and the house had become dilapidated over the years. One gutter was hanging off the eaves, and the windows were filthy with grime. Just as Mrs. Sanchez had said, the house was dark.

Ric made his way stealthily up the driveway and around to the backyard. Wading through knee-high weeds, he reached the rosebush and crouched down in front of it. Then he felt for the stone beneath the bush. As he brushed the leaves aside, he could feel the indentation of engraved letters. He took out his car keys. The key chain doubled as a flash-light. His heart pounded as he read the inscription: "In Loving Memory." *It really was Tony's grave!*

Ric didn't know how long he crouched in horror over the headstone. In his mind, he kept seeing Robles push Tony down the stairs. Then he saw the old man attacking Mr. Pike with his knife. He hated the old man and made up his mind that the next day he would go to the police. He owed it to Tony and to Mr. Pike. Finally, he got up and went home.

Ric glanced at the kitchen clock as he entered the back door. Ten-thirty. The house was quiet. Everyone had gone to bed. Up in his room there was a note on his pillow, written in Eva's handwriting. "Claudia called—three times! You're supposed to call her." But Ric didn't feel like talking to anyone. He undressed and climbed into bed.

That night Ric couldn't sleep. Every time he was about to doze off, the image of Tony's gravestone flashed into his mind. Finally around one o'clock, he got up, turned on his light, and opened his history book. He thought maybe reading might make him sleepy. Anyway, he'd developed a sort of interest in history lately.

As he lay there reading about Martin Van Buren, the president after Jackson, he heard his father moan from the next room. Probably having a bad dream, he thought. But a few minutes later he heard the moan again, this time louder. Ric went down the hall and looked into his parents' bedroom. They both seemed to be sleeping peacefully. Then Ric heard it again. His heart jumped as he realized the noise was coming from outside the house and that it was the same moaning sound he had heard over a week ago. This time there was no storm to blame it on.

Silently, he moved to the window in his parents' bedroom and looked out. From the attic window of the Robles' house, a light shone dimly through the shade. Robles is back! he thought. He stood in the darkness, watching and listening.

He heard the moaning again, louder than before. Then he saw a silhouette— the silhouette of a young man, a man with broad shoulders who held himself like a soldier—reflected on the shade. But just that quickly, the light went out, and the silhouette was gone.

Ric's heart pounded in his ears. What young visitor could Robles possibly have? he asked himself. But he already knew the answer. It had to be Tony. And Tony was dead. Ric had seen his grave that night. Mrs. Sanchez was right. The ghost of Tony Robles still haunted his father's house!

9 RIC WOKE UP to the sound of rain pounding on the roof. He sat up in bed and looked out the window. The rain was coming down in sheets, and the sky was filled with swirling gray clouds. It looked like it could rain all day. Good, Ric thought. We'll have a shortened practice tonight. Probably just watch some game films. I can go to the police station right afterward. He didn't look forward to that trip, but he knew he had to do it.

Claudia was waiting for him in American history.

"Ric, I've got great news!" she said excitedly. "I get to start practicing with the squad again. I talked to Mr. Adams, and he said I can do extra credit to bring my grades up. And when I told Mrs. McCall, the cheerleading sponsor, she said I could start practicing again. If I pass this course, I get my eligibility back at the quarter—just in time for the big games!"

Ric remembered Mr. Pike's comment about students using extra credit to bail themselves out. It sure applied in Claudia's case.

"Oh, Ricky, aren't you glad for me?"

"Yeah, it's great, Claudia. I'm real happy."

Claudia frowned. "Well, you could show a little more enthusiasm than that, Ric Salas. By the way, I called you last night. Why didn't you call me back? I wanted to tell you the big news as soon as I heard it."

Ric made up a quick excuse. "I didn't get home 'til late, and I thought maybe you'd be asleep."

"Oh, Ricky, you know you can call me any time." Claudia smiled sweetly. "But speaking of sleep, you don't look like you got much last night." At that moment, the bell rang, and Ric was relieved.

Mr. Adams proceeded with the day's discussion. Again, few of the students had read the assignment, so he did most of the talking. During class, Ric had the feeling that someone was staring at him. He looked over and saw Tina Lanza smiling at him. He smiled back. Then he glanced at Claudia. She had seen him smile at Tina and was scowling at him.

Ric was glad when lunch time came around. All morning, he'd found it hard to concentrate in his classes. He kept thinking about what he had seen the night before and the trip he had to make that afternoon.

"Can I sit with you?"

Ric looked up to see Tina.

"Sure," he said. "Have a seat."

"So, how's it going?" she asked, smiling.

"Okay, I guess," Ric answered. He looked at Tina closely for the first time. She had a pleasant face, a soft, light brown face, with friendly eyes and an engaging smile. That was what was different about her—her smile. It always seemed to be there. Or when it wasn't, it could be called up so easily. He had never seen her frown, or scowl, or glare coldly at anyone. She was like fresh air in a stuffy room.

"Just okay?" she asked.

No, not really okay, he thought. I just found out there's someone buried in the yard next to mine. I think I might be living next door to the person who attacked Mr. Pike. And for the first time in years, I find myself believing in ghosts. He longed to tell her these things. She looked like someone he could trust, someone who would understand. But before he got a chance, Claudia appeared.

"Oh, no," he said as he saw her approach. From the look on her face, she was obviously smoldering.

She marched over to their table, her hands on her hips.

"Tina, I've gotta talk to Ric—*alone!*" Claudia snapped.

Tina shrugged, picked up her tray, and moved to another table.

"What'd you do that for, Claudia?" Ric demanded. "That was rude."

"Are you dumping me, Ric, or what?" Claudia demanded.

Ric was surprised. "You dumped me, remember?" he said.

"But I thought we made up," Claudia said. Then a bitter look crossed her face. "Oh, I get it. This is payback time. Your feelings were hurt when I dumped you, and now you wanna give me a taste of my own medicine. So what now? Do I get down on my knees and beg your forgiveness?"

Ric sighed deeply. The last thing he needed was more conflict in his life. "Claudia," he said wearily, "I'm sorry, but I don't want to start dating again."

"Why not?" she demanded.

"In the last week or so, I've realized that you and I just don't see things the same way."

"Because I don't pretend to be all broken up over Pike?" Claudia asked harshly.

"It's more than that, Claudia. I just don't feel good about us anymore."

"So you're saying we're through, right?" Claudia asked, with sudden tears in her eyes.

"I'm sorry, Claudia," Ric said. "I really am."

Suddenly Claudia's mood changed. "You scumbag! You think you're better than I am, don't you?"

"Claudia, no, I never said that."

"You never said it, but that's what you were thinking! Mr. A-Student! You'll be

sorry for this, Ric Salas. Real sorry!"
Claudia spun around and marched away.

Ric continued to struggle to pay attention in his afternoon classes. Instead of
concentrating on his school work, he
began to think of excuses for not going to
the police. Maybe football practice would
last too long. And maybe his mother was
right. Maybe he should just mind his own
business. After all, he had no real proof
that Robles had attacked Mr. Pike. But
he couldn't deny the existence of the
gravestone—he'd seen it with his own
eyes. And the reflection on the shade. He
had to agree with Mrs. Sanchez.
Something wasn't right over there.

As Ric had predicted, practice was
shortened that night. The coach ran them
through a few calisthenics, showed them
a couple of game films, and let them go.

After practice, Ric drove downtown. He
parked his car, fed the parking meter, and
ran through the rain to the police station.
He entered the big double doors of the
building and walked across the marble
floor to the front desk. The officer on duty
looked up as Ric approached. His badge

read "Sergeant Ron Lee."

"Can I help you?" the sergeant asked.

"Yes. I'd like to see Officer Thomas," Ric said.

"What is your name, son?" Sergeant Lee wanted to know.

"Ric. Ric Salas."

"All right, Ric. I'm Sergeant Lee. Now, what do you want to see Officer Thomas about?"

"It's about the Pike case," Ric explained. "I've got some information I think she should know about."

"What kind of information?" the sergeant wanted to know.

Ric hesitated. He didn't feel comfortable telling everyone about his suspicions. "Um, I'd rather not discuss it with anyone but Officer Thomas," he said.

Sergeant Lee looked doubtful, but he picked up the phone and pressed a few buttons. Then he said, "Thomas? A Ric Salas is here to see you. Says he has some information about the stabbing Friday night." He hung up the phone.

"Officer Thomas will be here in a minute. You can wait over there," the sergeant said, nodding at some chairs that lined the wall a few feet away.

Ric sat down and waited. The station was a busy place. The big double doors opened and closed every few seconds. It seemed that people from all walks of life passed through them—police officers, men and women dressed in business attire, average-looking people, homeless people. As he watched the people come and go, Ric wondered if any of them were as nervous as he was. His throat was so dry it was an effort to swallow, and his palms were warm and sweaty.

"Hello, Ric," a female voice said.

Ric looked up to see the police officer he had talked to the night Mr. Pike was stabbed. She smiled and extended her hand in a friendly manner.

"Hi, Officer Thomas," he said. As he shook her hand, he hoped she wouldn't notice how nervous he was.

"Nice to see you again, Ric," she said. "Come on. We'll go to my desk."

Officer Thomas led Ric through the front lobby and into a large room with a maze of desks. At almost every desk there was a police officer, a typewriter, and stacks of paperwork. Some of the officers were interviewing people. Others were typing or shuffling through the papers on their desks. A few officers looked up and nodded as Ric passed.

"Have a seat," Officer Thomas said. She pointed to a gray metal chair at the end of her desk. "Coffee? Soda?"

"No, thanks," said Ric, sitting down.

"Now, Ric, Officer Lee tells me you have some information regarding the Pike case. Is that right?"

"Yes," said Ric, swallowing hard.

"Okay, I'm listening," said Officer Thomas, leaning back and chewing on the end of her pen. Ric noticed that she was watching him closely, as if looking for signs of what kind of person he might be.

Ric hesitated. He suddenly felt silly for being there. It had been a bad idea after all, he decided. How could he possibly tell this intelligent young woman that he had seen a ghost next door? She and the other officers would laugh him right out of the station.

"Ric?" Officer Thomas said. "What did you want to tell me?"

He decided to skip the ghost part and just tell her about the gravestone. He took a deep breath and began.

"I think someone is buried in the backyard of the house next door to mine," he said at last. "The Robles' house."

Officer Thomas looked surprised. "Excuse me?" she said.

Ric bit his bottom lip. He noticed that a few of the typewriters around him had stopped. Were the other officers listening? He decided to press on. After all, he had seen Tony's grave and had read the inscription on it. It was real.

"I said I think someone is buried in the backyard of the Robles' house."

Officer Thomas had a perplexed look on her face. "Why do you think that, Ric?"

"Because I saw the gravestone. I even read what it said—'In Loving Memory.'" He was certain now—the room was much quieter than when he had come in. The other officers were listening. They probably think I'm crazy, he thought.

"Just where is this gravestone, Ric?"

"Under a rosebush. It's kind of hard to see. Old man—I mean, Mr. Robles keeps it covered with leaves and grass and stuff."

"How did you happen to see it, then?" Officer Thomas asked.

"I was up late one night studying. Right before I went to bed, I glanced out my bedroom window. I saw Mr. Robles in his backyard. He was kneeling in front of the rosebush."

"And?"

"I watched him for a minute. The moon was real bright that night, and I could see something gleaming on the ground under the bush. It looked like a gravestone. Mr. Robles covered it with leaves and stuff before he went in the house."

"And you could read what it said from your bedroom window?"

"No. Last night I decided to take a closer look. So I sneaked into the Robles' yard and shined a flashlight on the stone. That's when I saw the inscription."

"Was there any name on this…gravestone?" Officer Thomas asked.

"No," said Ric.

"Let me ask you a question, Ric. Who

do you think is buried there?"

Ric glanced around. Some of the other officers looked down quickly when his eyes met theirs. Others continued to stare at him in an odd way. They do think I'm crazy, he thought. I guess I can't blame them. But I started this, so I might as well finish it, he decided. He took another deep breath and said, "I think Tony Robles is buried there."

"Tony Robles?" Officer Thomas asked, obviously surprised. From where he sat, Ric could hear several officers chuckling. "But Tony Robles disappeared years ago. He ran away one night and has never been seen again. His case is closed."

"I know that's the story," Ric said. "But I think he's buried in his backyard."

"I see," said Officer Thomas. "And who do you think buried him there, Ric?"

"His father—Carlos Robles," Ric answered.

Ric thought he saw a hint of amusement in Officer Thomas' eyes. Despite this, he continued.

"I know it sounds crazy, but it's true. Don't you see? Mr. Robles just told the police that Tony ran away. I think when Mr. Robles pushed Tony down the stairs that night, he accidentally killed him. Then he buried Tony in the backyard."

"Ric, that's an awfully serious accusation to make against anyone."

"I know, but it's true. I swear it is. It all makes sense now. Robles has been covering up the murder for ten years."

"But, Ric, you said you had information about the Pike case. What does what you've just told me have to do with the stabbing last Friday night?"

Ric looked around again. Some of the officers were still smiling. Well, they can laugh all they want, Ric thought. But Carlos Robles is an evil old man who needs to pay for what he's done.

"I think Carlos Robles stabbed Mr. Pike," he said.

This time Officer Thomas looked more than surprised—she was stunned. "But, Ric, why would Mr. Robles do that? What motive could he possibly have? I questioned Mr. Pike today, and he said he didn't even know Mr. Robles."

"I'm not sure. But I think he thought Mr.

Pike was a detective or something."

"Why would he jump to that conclusion?" the policewoman wanted to know.

"You remember that night I saw him in his backyard...by the rosebush?" Ric asked.

"Yes."

"Well, he saw me watching him, and he knows I saw the gravestone. He probably thinks I called the police that night and told them what I saw, so they sent someone over to investigate. He thought Mr. Pike was that someone."

Officer Thomas shook her head. "I have to tell you, Ric, that's some story."

She doesn't believe me, he thought. "I know it sounds crazy, but could you at least check it out?" He had to get them over there. They had to see the gravestone.

Officer Thomas smiled and nodded. "I think we can do that, Ric. But you might as well know, I've been trying to reach Mr. Robles since Friday night. He seems to have left town."

"I think he's home now," Ric said.

"Oh, did you see him?" Officer Thomas

wanted to know.

Ric hesitated. "Not exactly," he said. "But I saw a light on at the house."

"Good. Maybe he's back, then. I'll go over there tomorrow. In the meantime, don't spread any of this around, okay? You don't want Mr. Robles suing you for slander." She stood up then and offered her hand across the desk. "Thanks so much for coming, Ric."

"You're welcome," Ric said, shaking her hand again.

"Can you find your way out?" Officer Thomas asked.

"Yeah, no problem." As Ric made his way through the maze of desks, he avoided looking at any of the officers. He didn't want to see the amused looks on their faces.

On the way home, Ric stopped off at the hospital. He was relieved to find out that Mr. Pike had made it through the last twenty-four hours. In fact, the young teacher had been taken out of intensive care and moved to a regular room. His condition had been upgraded to serious. Ric was allowed to see him for a few minutes.

As he entered the room, he saw Mrs. Pike sitting at the bedside. She was holding Mr. Pike's hand and talking to him in a quiet voice.

"Hi, Mr. Pike," Ric said softly.

"Ric," Mr. Pike said. "It's good to see you."

"It's great seeing you," Ric said. "I'm glad you're better."

"Thanks," the teacher said. Ric noticed that Mr. Pike's voice sounded weak. "It was touch-and-go for a while," Mr. Pike continued. "Lots of prayers and medical skill. Doctors say I might even be able to go home in a couple of weeks. Then I'll have to take it easy for a while."

"Do you remember much about that night, Mr. Pike?" Ric asked.

Mr. Pike took a shaky breath. "Not much," he said. "In fact, the police were here to see me today. I'm afraid I wasn't much help. I remember trying to rouse Mr. Robles at the front door…then I went around to the back. And the next thing I knew, I felt this incredible pain in my back. I guess I stumbled into the alley and collapsed."

Ric had to know if Mr. Pike had seen the gravestone. "So you didn't see anything unusual that night?" he asked.

"No, it was pretty dark. I didn't even hear anyone come up behind me, and I've got pretty good hearing."

Ric knew that for a fact. Mr. Pike could hear the slightest whisper in class.

The teacher smiled and shook his head. "It must have been a ghost or something," he said. "Nothing else could sneak up on me that way."

He saw the shocked look on Ric's face. "Hey, I'm only kidding, Ric," he added, still smiling. "Seriously though, they tell me if you hadn't found me, I would have bled to death. I owe you my life."

Ric blushed. It was unusual to hear a teacher say he owed a student something. "I'm just glad I found you, Mr. Pike."

"So am I," Mr. Pike said, gazing at his wife. "So am I."

Ric left the hospital feeling good. Mr. Pike would be all right. And Ric had gone to see Officer Thomas. The worst was behind him.

Now all he had to do was convince the

police that old man Robles had attacked Mr. Pike. It was obvious they weren't going to simply take Ric's word for it. He needed more evidence, something that would incriminate Robles in the stabbing of Mr. Pike.

As he drove home, the thought came to him. He would have to return to the scene of the crime. Why hadn't he thought of this before? He'd start by looking around the alley behind his house.

By the time Ric reached Linden Street, the rain had stopped, but it was still quite windy, and the sun had set. He knew it would be better to wait until daylight, but it wouldn't hurt to have a quick look around now.

Ric parked his car in the same place behind the garage. He shined his head-lights down the alley, just as he had done the night Mr. Pike had been stabbed. Then he walked over to where the young teacher had fallen. The gravel was no longer stained with blood. The rain had taken care of that.

He started to look around for clues—something Robles might have dropped or something unusual in the area. Suddenly he saw a large dark figure moving up the alley toward him.

Ric shrank back, thinking of the *aparecido*. A cold current shot up his spine. The figure moved noiselessly. Ric considered running when suddenly he heard his name.

"Salas?" the figure said.

Ric recognized the voice and breathed a sigh of relief. It was Rafe. Big, hulking, sullen Rafe but better than a ghost any day. Or at least he hoped so.

"Yeah," Ric answered.

Rafe stopped a few yards off. "This where you found Pike?" he asked.

"Uh huh," Ric said.

"Did he say anything to you...like if he saw who attacked him?" Rafe asked.

"No," Ric shook his head. "He was unconscious."

Rafe moved closer. "You know, the cops came to my house to talk to me, Salas. You been running off at the mouth about that blade I carry?" His voice had turned menacing.

"I didn't tell the cops anything about you," Ric said. "But everybody knows how steamed you and Stan were about getting bounced from the team. The cops probably talked to Stan too."

Rafe came even closer. Now he was only about two feet away. The light from the headlights cast a weird shadow across his face. "Hey, I'm already on probation from that fight last year. I'm not gonna end up in some kind of lockup, man."

Ric backed up. "I didn't tell them anything about you," he repeated.

"How do I know that for sure? You lied before, Salas," Rafe said, moving closer. "And I'll bet you're lying now. You probably told the cops all kinds of things about me."

"You got the wrong guy, Rafe," Ric insisted. "I'm telling you." He backed up some more, but suddenly he was against the chain-link fence that enclosed his backyard.

Rafe stood only a foot or so in front of Ric. Suddenly he grabbed the front of Ric's jacket and thrust his face into Ric's. "You sweatin', you little weasel? Tell me what you told the cops."

"Nothing. I swear," Ric insisted.

Ric's heart was pounding in his chest. Rafe meant business. Ric knew that no matter what he said, Rafe would never believe that he hadn't told the police about the knife. Especially since Ric had lied about his talk with the principal. So Ric would have to take Rafe on. And this wasn't the football field.

On the field, Ric could hit the other padded players with everything he had. Rarely did anyone get hurt seriously. He didn't know if he could do the same off the field. He had never really fought anyone before and wasn't sure he wanted to start now.

Suddenly Rafe struck. Ric felt as if he had been hit in the stomach with a cannonball. He doubled over, gasping for breath. Then Rafe hit him again, this time with an uppercut to the jaw. The force of the blow snapped Ric's head back. As he hit the ground, he felt gravel cut into his hand.

"Go ahead," Rafe said, breathing heavily. "Catch your breath. I'm not done with you yet."

Ric sat dazed for a few seconds. The pain was almost overwhelming. He staggered to his feet and lunged at Rafe, but the bigger boy was ready for him. Rafe jerked his knee up and caught Ric square in the chest, throwing him backwards. Chain links rattled loudly as Ric flew into the fence. Rafe waited, poised for the fight.

As Ric dragged himself to his feet again, he spotted his father's old rake leaning against the inside of the fence. He reached back and snatched it up.

Rafe wasn't expecting a rake in his face. With all his strength, Ric brought the head of the rake down, leaving a nasty gouge in Rafe's cheek.

Rafe could send big football players flying with his rushing attack. Now he came at Ric, his eyes on fire. With incredible force, he knocked the rake from Ric's hands. Before Ric knew what had happened, Rafe had him pinned to the ground.

Rafe grabbed Ric's throat with his huge hands and began to squeeze. Ric gasped for breath, struggling in vain against the weight and strength of Rafe. Then things started to go dark. But just as he was on the verge of passing out, Ric felt the weight being lifted from his chest. Rafe's grip loosened on his throat, and Ric could breathe again. Is that it? Ric wondered. Did he just want to scare me?

He propped himself up on his elbows just in time to see Rafe hurtling backwards through the beams of the headlights. It was then that Ric realized someone else was in the alley. Could his father have heard the commotion and come to his rescue? he wondered. But Joe Salas was not a big man. He could never have handled someone like Rafe so easily.

"What the—" Ric heard Rafe exclaim.

Ric could see Rafe sitting on the ground a few feet away. The beam from one of the headlights shined on him like a spotlight. Someone was standing in the shadows nearby. Rafe had a wild look of fear on his face. Then, like a huge rat, he scrambled away into the darkness.

Immediately, the man turned to Ric. In the shadows, Ric could vaguely see his features. He was clean-shaven with short, dark hair. Other than that, Ric could only tell that the man was tall with an athletic build. Whoever he is, Ric thought, he must be incredibly strong.

Ric was about to say thanks when the man crossed in front of the beams. Ric stared openmouthed. The shoulders. The way the man carried himself—straight as a soldier. Suddenly Ric realized it wasn't a man at all. Heading toward him was the ghost of Tony Robles!

10

RIC WANTED TO run for home as fast as he could. But curiosity and fear held him rigid. He stared at the ghost with the kind of fascination that draws people to horrendous sights.

"Are you all right?" the ghost asked.

Ric nodded. "You're—you're Tony Robles," he stammered.

"Yes," he said. "I am Tony Robles." Ric detected a note of sadness in his voice.

"But you've been dead for..." Ric's voice trailed off.

"The last ten years?" the ghost asked. He nodded his head. "You could say that."

Ric couldn't believe his ears. He was having a conversation with a ghost!

"I've heard you...late at night," Ric stammered.

The ghost shook his head. "That was my father you heard," he said.

"Your father? I don't understand," said Ric, getting to his feet.

"No, I wouldn't expect you to," said Tony's ghost.

Ric tried again. "Your father said you were only hurt and you ran away. He lied, then?"

"My father doesn't lie," said the ghost.

Now Ric was really confused. If Robles didn't lie, then Tony really did run away. "But if you ran away—"

"Then I can't be dead," said the ghost.

Ric gasped with the realization. This was not the ghost of Tony Robles. This was Tony Robles, back after ten years!

"When did you get back?" Ric asked.

Tony Robles looked at the ground and sighed deeply. "I was never gone."

"Never gone? Then your father did lie."

"I told you—my father doesn't lie," Tony said quickly. "But I do." He paused. "And it's time I stopped." He seemed to be talking to himself.

Suddenly he looked straight at Ric. "You are the boy who lives here?"

"Yes," said Ric. "I'm Ric Salas."

"Then you've probably heard all the stories and the rumors."

Ric nodded. "I've heard that you and

your father fought a lot."

"That's true. We did fight," Tony admitted. "I'm ashamed to say just how much we fought."

"He didn't want you to play football, right?" Ric asked. He knew that had to be the reason.

"No," Tony said, "actually just the opposite. I had a scholarship to the state university, a football scholarship. Books, tuition, everything. My father couldn't afford to send me to college on a fisherman's wages, and it was my mother's dying wish that I go. My father loved her deeply. He wanted to carry out her wishes. He knew that the only way I would get to college would be on that scholarship. So he told me I had to go."

"And you didn't want to?" Ric asked, surprised.

"No," Tony said simply.

"But why?" Ric asked. "You were an outstanding running back. You could have had a great career."

"Yeah, I was good at football. But I didn't love the game, not the way some guys do. I wanted to be what my father was, a fisherman. And that's why we fought."

For a while, Tony was quiet, seemingly lost in thought. Ric could hear a dog barking in the neighborhood and an occasional car door slam. Finally, Ric reminded him, "You were telling me about that night."

"Oh, yes, that night," Tony said. "My father and I had been fighting a lot. I was nearing the end of my senior year in high school, and I had to commit to the university or lose my scholarship. My father was putting a lot of pressure on me." He looked at Ric. "Have you ever wanted something very badly? And then have someone tell you that you can't have it? Do you know how that feels?"

"Yeah, I think so," Ric said, thinking of his fights with his own father.

"Finally, I couldn't stand it any longer. I told my father that if he made me go away to college, I would run away the first chance I got. He started yelling at me, 'No, you won't! You will not, Tony Robles!'

"We were up in my bedroom. I stormed past him to go downstairs. I needed to get out of the house for awhile—to get away from him. I told him he was a stupid old man, who didn't understand anything. He followed me, still yelling.

"As I headed down the stairs, he tried to grab me, to keep me from leaving. I pushed him away...he lost his balance and..." Tony buried his face in his hands.

"*You* pushed your *father* down the stairs?" Ric asked incredulously.

"I didn't mean to. It was an accident. I never meant to hurt him."

"What happened then?" Ric asked.

"When he reached the bottom of the stairs, he just lay there all crumpled up. He never moved a muscle. I ran to him and turned him over. His eyes were open, and he was struggling to talk. But he couldn't seem to form the words. I knew something was wrong, seriously wrong. I got him into bed and stayed at his bedside all night. He never moved. His eyes were open, but he never moved.

"The next day, I thought he might be better." Tony shook his head. "I was just a kid. What did I know? But he wasn't better the next day. Or the next, or the next. That's when I realized the fall had permanently paralyzed him."

Poor Mr. Robles, Ric thought. And here all this time I thought he had pushed Tony down the stairs.

"Did you take him to the hospital or call an ambulance or anything?" Ric asked.

Tony shook his head. "How could I? How could I tell anyone what I had done to my own father? I knew if I did, they would take him away from me and put him in a hospital somewhere. And me? They would have sent me to a juvenile detention center, maybe even prison."

He stopped for a moment, thinking. "No," he continued, "I made up my mind that my father was my responsibility. I had caused his injury, so I should take care of him. And that is what I have done for ten years."

"But your father is fine," said Ric. "I've seen him many times. He goes to work. I've seen him in the yard—"

"You've seen me, not my father," Tony said.

Ric was now totally confused. "You? But…"

"Ten years ago, I became my father,"

Tony said. "I let my hair grow long and grew a beard. I wore a hat over my face. I withdrew from people. No one ever got close enough to know it wasn't Carlos."

"But why?"

"I knew if I remained Tony, there would be questions about where my father was. So I became my father and claimed that Tony had run away. It made sense that a kid would run away, especially after all the fighting."

"But where is your father?" Ric asked. "Where is Carlos?"

"I fixed a room for him in the attic, away from the world. That's where I care for him."

"Then the moaning I've heard—" Ric began.

"Was the moaning of a pitiful old man," said Tony. "A man who can't move or speak."

And the silhouette he and Mrs. Sanchez had seen. It really *was* Tony, Ric thought.

"Wait a minute," said Ric. "The police searched your house ten years ago. Why didn't they find your father?"

Tony shrugged. "I built a false wall in

the attic and moved his bed behind it. Then, the day I called the police to report Tony missing, I gave my father a harmless sleeping pill. He slept soundly through the whole search."

Ric was still puzzled. "But why did you call the police?"

"I knew eventually there would be questions—where was Tony, why didn't he ever come home? I decided to clear it up before the questions started. The police were suspicious at first. I expected them to be. But I was pretty sure that eventually they would declare Tony as a missing person since they wouldn't be able to find a body. And that's what they did."

"But ten years? How could you stand it? You were a young man, you still are. You gave up your life."

"In a way, yes. But in another way, no. I actually got part of the life I wanted. I became a fisherman."

Ric looked at Tony. He looked nothing like the person Ric had seen next door all these years.

"Why did you decide to reveal your true self tonight?" Ric asked.

Tony took a deep breath. "Last Friday I saw the attack on the teacher."

"You *saw* Mr. Pike stabbed?" Ric cried. "Who was it? Who attacked him? What did he look like?"

"I only saw him from behind," Tony said, "and it was dark. He had on a green coat—like an Army coat. And he had long black hair."

Rafe! Long black hair! So it *was* him. "Why didn't you call the police?" Ric demanded.

"I know you'll find this hard to understand, but I didn't want to get involved. I was afraid my identity would be discovered. So I parked my truck at the docks and took a taxi home. Then I turned off all the lights in the house and pretended not to be home. The police have been here many times, but they think I'm gone.

"While I was hiding in the house, I began thinking about what I had become. I was too cowardly to help another person. I left that teacher to die. Do you see what living a lie has done to me? So tonight I decided to put an end to it. I made up my mind to tell the police what I had seen Friday night. And what I had done ten years ago. If they put me in prison, it won't be any worse than the prison I've kept myself in all these years.

"So I shaved my beard and cut my hair. I threw away the hat. I was just calling a taxi to take me to my truck when I heard the commotion in the alley. That's when I saw you being attacked—by the same person who had attacked the teacher. He didn't have that green coat on, but the hair looked the same. I should have chased him down, but I wasn't sure how badly you were hurt. I couldn't desert you—not like I deserted the teacher last Friday."

"So what will you do now?" Ric asked.

"I'm still going to the police. Not just for myself, but for my father too. I see now that he should be in a hospital. He's ten years older, and his body is weaker. He needs more care than I can give him."

"I could go with you," Ric volunteered. He figured they'd probably want to talk to him anyway once Tony told them about the attack tonight.

"Thanks," said Tony. "But this is something I have to do myself. So if you're okay,

I guess I'll get going." He turned to go.

Something had been bothering Ric, gnawing at the back of his mind during his conversation with Tony. Now he realized what it was.

"Wait! Tony!" he called. "The rose-bush—whose grave is underneath the rosebush?"

"Grave?" Tony asked, obviously surprised.

"Yeah, I saw your father, I mean I saw you kneeling by it that night you saw me in the window. And I was over there just last night. There's a gravestone with an inscription on it—'In Loving Memory.' If you're alive, and your father's alive, who's buried there?"

"No one's buried there," Tony said. "My father planted that rosebush when my mother died—as a memorial. Sometimes I visit the rosebush. It makes me very sad, but it also makes me feel closer to a mother I never really knew."

Ric watched Tony leave. Unbelievable, he thought. Here I've been living next door to him all this time and never even knew it. This will sure give Mrs. Sanchez something to talk about.

He walked over to his car and started the engine. Then he drove around to Linden Street. As he entered his driveway, he saw a taxi pull up next door and Tony get in.

"Good luck, Tony," Ric whispered.

He parked his car and went into the house. As he passed through the living room, his parents looked up in horror. His jaw was swollen, and his clothes were muddy. "Ricky!" his mother cried. "What happened?"

"I'll tell you in a minute, Mom," he said, not stopping. "Right now I have to make a phone call."

He went up to his room and called the police station. He asked to be put through to Officer Thomas. Ric told her about his fight with Rafe in the alley.

"I was wrong, Officer Thomas," he said. "Mr. Robles had nothing to do with the attack on Mr. Pike. It was Rafe Thompson all along."

Officer Thomas wanted to take Ric's statement in person. She told him she would be at his house in a few minutes.

As he hung up the phone, he heard honking outside. He looked out the window. A car was entering the driveway.

Claudia, he sighed, recognizing her car. What now?

Ric went downstairs and out to Claudia's car. The window was down. "Claudia, what're you doing here?" he asked.

"I need to talk to you," she said, getting out of her car. She had her blue and white cheerleading outfit on. Even in the dim glow of the street light, Ric could see her trim, muscular legs. Suddenly she noticed his injuries. "Ric, what happened?" she cried, touching his swollen jaw.

"Nothing. It's no big deal, really." He brushed her hand away. "What did you want to talk to me about?"

"Oh, Ric, I acted so dumb yesterday in the cafeteria. I came to apologize," Claudia said.

"It's all right, Claudia. Don't worry about it."

"Can you forgive me?"

"Sure. You're forgiven," Ric said. He started to turn to go when he felt her hand on his shoulder.

"It's just that I care so much for you…" Claudia continued, turning him around. "You know I do."

Ric gently removed her hand. "Claudia, we're just friends, remember?"

This time she put a hand on both shoulders.

"Oh, Ricky, I've missed you so much these last few days," she purred.

Ric gently disengaged her hands. "Claudia…" he said.

Claudia smiled and returned her hands to his shoulders. "Come on, baby. You can't resist me. You never could before." She stroked his neck gently with the tips of her fingers.

Ric drew away, shaking his head. "No, Claudia. Stop. It's not going to work for us anymore. "

Suddenly she began to cry. "Oh, Ricky," she said between sobs. "Don't you see? I don't want to lose you. You're everything to me."

"Claudia, I'm not so special," said Ric. "All kinds of guys would like to go out with you. Give it a few days. You'll be dating someone else soon, and then you'll forget all about me. Now, come on. It's time you went home."

He opened her car door and gently guided her into the car. The dome light threw a soft light onto the seats. It was then that Ric saw the olive green Army coat in the backseat.

"Claudia, have you been hanging out with Rafe?" he asked.

"Why?" she asked hopefully. "Would that make you jealous?"

"No. I just wondered why his coat is in your backseat. I mean…it looks like his coat," Ric said.

"That coat belongs to my dad," Claudia said quickly. "He must have left it in here when he used my car the other night."

Ric noticed that her crying had stopped as quickly as it had begun.

"Oh, Ric," she continued, looking up at him from the driver's seat. "Remember how good we were together? You sure you want to give that up?"

Ric was silent. His mind was racing.

Claudia mistook his silence for uncertainty. "You don't have to tell me tonight, Ric. Just think about it. That's all I'm asking you to do. Okay?"

Ric's heart had begun to pound madly. He stared at the tall, muscular girl. She was about five feet ten inches and was as strong as any young man that size. Her long, lustrous hair flowed down her back like black ribbons. In the dark—in that olive green trench coat—she could easily have been mistaken for a young man.

Ric took a desperate chance. "Claudia, I saw Mr. Pike today…he told me he saw who attacked him."

"He couldn't have," Claudia cried, too quickly.

"Why not, Claudia?" Ric asked.

"Because—he was stabbed in the back—" Her lower lip trembled.

"And Mr. Pike said the attacker had on a big olive green coat. And had long, dark hair." Ric leaned into the open window. "Did you steal Rafe's knife at the football game?" he asked.

Claudia slammed the door shut and reached for the ignition keys.

"Not so fast, Claudia!" Ric said, reaching through the open window and grabbing both of her hands.

"Let me go!" Claudia screamed, struggling and kicking. Her strength amazed him, and he knew he could not hold her in this awkward position for long. Suddenly he let go of one hand and snatched the keys out of the ignition. Then he stepped back from the car, just out of her reach.

"Don't do this, Ricky. Don't do this to me!" she cried hysterically. "I'll give you anything, anything!" She laid her head on the steering wheel and began sobbing again. It was obvious to Ric that this time the tears were real.

After a minute she looked up. Tears were streaming down her cheeks. "Don't you see, Ric? I did it for you."

Ric was stunned. "What do you mean, you did it for me?"

"I told you before," Claudia said. "Pike wasn't good for you. He would have kept you from getting your scholarship. I couldn't let him do that. So last Friday at the Pizza Zone, I borrowed Rafe's coat. I told him I had to run out to my car for a minute and didn't want to get cold. I had seen him put his knife in his pocket at the game. And then I drove here…"

"But how did you know Mr. Pike would be in this neighborhood?" Ric asked.

"I have him for publications class, remember? He told us he was going to interview the old man after the game that night."

Ric felt sick. Claudia was so cold about what she had done.

"Oh, Ricky, I love you so!" Claudia pleaded. "Please let me go. I'll burn the coat—I'll deny everything. It's not too late for us. Please, Ricky." She was sobbing uncontrollably.

As Ric watched her, he knew that Claudia had lied. She hadn't attacked Pike for him. She had done it for herself—for her precious cheerleading.

Ric glanced up the street. In the distance, he could see a squad car heading up Linden toward his house. "No, Claudia. It *is* too late. Too late for us and too late for you."

The squad car pulled into Ric's driveway behind Claudia's car. Officer Thomas got out.

"Ric," she said. "I came as soon as I could."

Ric cleared his throat. "Um…Officer Thomas…you're not going to believe this, but—"

Ric explained everything to the policewoman while Claudia sat sobbing in the car.

Officer Thomas examined Rafe's coat and found blood spots on it. Taking the coat, she helped Claudia out of the car and led her to the squad car. As they drove away, Ric could see Claudia in the backseat, her head down and her long black hair covering her face.

"Good-bye, Claudia," he said sadly.

* * *

The next day, an ambulance came to take Mr. Robles away. Ric watched as the paramedics wheeled the old man down the driveway and into the big vehicle. Tony was by his side the whole time. From where Ric stood, the old man looked small and frail. I hope the doctors will be able to help him, Ric thought.

As Ric watched the ambulance pull away, he saw Tony heading toward the Salas' house. Ric met him at the front door and stepped out onto the porch.

"I wanted to stop by before I left today," said Tony.

"How's your father?" Ric asked.

"They won't know until they run some tests on him. We should know something by the end of the week."

"I hope he's all right," Ric said.

"Thanks," said Tony. "And thanks for offering to go to the police station with me last night."

"No problem," said Ric. "How did it go?"

"Actually, pretty good," Tony replied. "They seemed to believe me when I told them what happened that night. They have a few more questions they want to ask me, but it doesn't sound like they're going to press charges against me."

"That's great," said Ric. "Then you can stay in close touch with your father."

"Yeah, I hope to be able to bring him back home eventually."

"So you'd continue to live in your house then?" Ric asked.

"Sure," Tony said. "It's the only home I've ever known. Well, I'd better go. I want to be there when my father is checked into his room. Thanks again, Ric."

"You're welcome," Ric said. "Oh, and Tony. I've got something of yours."

"Something of mine?" Tony asked.

Ric removed the chain he was wearing from his neck. Then he slipped the bronze medallion off and held it out for Tony to see.

"Yeah. My little brother found this," Ric said. "I've been wearing it for good luck."

Tony's eyes widened as he took the medallion from Ric's hand. "I haven't seen this in years," he said, smiling.

"Well, it's yours," said Ric. "So you can have it back."

Tony shook his head. "No, you keep it, Ric," he said. "That part of my life is over. I'm not the same Tony Robles I was then." He handed the medallion back to Ric. "If it brings you luck, be my guest," Tony said, turning to go.

"Gee, thanks," said Ric.

Ric watched Tony cross the yard, get into his old truck, and drive away.

It'll be weird having real neighbors next door, Ric thought—neighbors he could wave to or talk to. But it would be nice too.

"Welcome back to the neighborhood, Tony," Ric said, closing the door. Ric headed for the dining room. He had homework to do.